An Accidental

Scandal

A PRIDE AND PREJUDICE NOVELLA

MELANIE RACHEL

Contents

Chapter One

The play was over.

Elizabeth realized, with a shock, that she and Aunt Gardiner had spoken over nearly the entire final act. It was unlike her to converse during a performance; she visited the theatre so rarely that the entertainment was always her first object.

She had only one night in London before she continued her journey into Kent, and she had wasted it. Had it been necessary to canvas Mr. Darcy's cruelty to Mr. Wickham and the latter man's subsequent engagement to the wealthy Miss King? Surely they might have spoken of it some other time. She was thoroughly disappointed in herself.

Aunt Gardiner had warned her not to become bitter, and truly, she was not. Mr. Darcy was free to disapprove of whomever he chose, and Mr. Wickham likewise free to find his fortune where he might.

Of the two, however, she must give Mr. Darcy his due. Begrudgingly, perhaps, but her aunt's gentle remonstrance reminded Elizabeth that she was not being fair. Very well, she would judge both men by their actions.

As unpleasant as he often was, Mr. Darcy had always been consistent. He might feel himself above them all, but there had at least been no dishonesty there. It pained Elizabeth to think it, but she could not say as much for Mr. Wickham, for he had neatly dropped the acquaintance of nearly every other lady the instant Miss King's inheritance became known.

Fortunately, it was but the work of a moment to remind herself that Mr. Wickham's circumstances were Mr. Darcy's fault.

There. Her world was set aright.

Perhaps it ought to make her feel better, having someone upon whom to place the blame, but it did not. Despite defending Mr. Wickham's engagement to her aunt, Elizabeth could not be satisfied with him. She was not in love with the man—he was too free with his flirtations for her to take him seriously in that way—but she did count him a friend, and for him to act in the same way Charlotte had . . . Well, Elizabeth thought ruefully, perhaps she herself was the one who was out of step.

After Charlotte had accepted an offer of marriage from the Bennets' ridiculous cousin Mr. Collins, Elizabeth's sister Jane had pointed out that not all people were the same. And it was true. All around her, people were making matches for security, for consequence. Perhaps she was the greater fool in waiting for a man she could admire and respect. Security was necessary, of course, but she would not accept an offer for safety alone. She feared and most emphatically did not want a marriage like that of her parents.

She wished for a marriage like the one the Gardiners shared. She wished for it very much.

Perhaps some would condemn her for rejecting Mr. Collins's offer of marriage last autumn. He was the heir to Longbourn, after all. Trading the security of Mr. Collins's situation for her sanity would have been a very poor bargain.

Everyone stood to gather their things as the throngs below began to make their way out to the lobby. Elizabeth's head ached, and she stepped out of the stuffy box before her companions, turning to her right and walking down the hall to peer down the grand marble staircase.

It was suitably wide, but she wondered whether a mistake had been made in the construction, for the treads were a little shallow and the whole quite steep. She felt a sickly flutter in her stomach as she always did when she was too close to the edge of something very high, and she stepped back. Thank goodness they were only in one of the lower boxes and not in the upper, where the very wealthy preferred to sit.

Then, because she detested feeling intimidated, she walked half a dozen steps to cross the hall and peered over the railing to the ground floor. She swallowed and forced herself to look, just as she had forced herself to climb trees as a girl.

The floor seemed very far down.

Her uncle had secured a larger box than normal this evening in deference to their party's size, but he need not have troubled himself; Sir William and Maria Lucas had politely declined the invitation. Elizabeth had never believed Sir William a man of much delicacy, but there too, she must have been mistaken. From something he had said quietly to Maria, Elizabeth learned he was offering her the gift of time with her family.

Though Jane's spirits were not what they had been before Mr. Bingley came into their lives, they had improved since Christmas. Her sister had not grown gaunt, nor was she eschewing company. That Jane harboured regrets was clear, but she would recover.

Elizabeth could not have travelled to Kent on the morrow had it been otherwise.

She sighed. At least she had correctly judged Miss Bingley to be a false friend to Jane. She had not been wrong about *that*. Elizabeth was vastly relieved.

That is, until a familiar voice broke into her contemplations.

"Miss Bennet!"

A terrible foreboding seized her as she turned to face the man who had spoken her name. And there he was, as though Elizabeth's own uncharitable thoughts had summoned him—Mr. Darcy.

The gentleman stood as still as a statue, only a few feet from her and appearing every bit as stunned as she was herself. Of all the men in London!

Elizabeth glanced down the hall to her family's box, judging the distance. Why, why had she stepped outside before everyone else? What could be keeping them?

Mr. Darcy had been the first person down the stairs from the upper boxes, but as he approached her, others were wandering down now. Some nodded at acquaintances or stopped to speak with them. Most made directly for the stairs nearest her. The hall, however, was filling with people as Mr. Darcy stepped up to greet her.

"Have you been separated from your party, Miss Bennet?" Mr. Darcy asked, almost solicitously. The tone of his voice was at odds with his stoic expression.

"Oh, no," she said. "I merely stepped out of our box before them, expecting that they should follow. However, they seem to have been detained."

"I see," he said, glancing down the stairs. He appeared to be searching for someone. "Please remain here. I shall return to await them with you."

"That is unnecessary," she said, but she was speaking to his broad back. She had meant to assure him that she did not require a chaperone, that she might simply step back inside the box and rejoin her family. Only she could not be so rude as to disappear before he returned, and with so many people now crowding the hall, a dozen feet might as well be a mile. How many people these boxes had held!

Mr. Darcy moved gracefully down about half of the stairs, where he stopped and spoke a few words in another man's ear. He then started back up to her, nodding to a few acquaintances along the way.

Not far behind her, a man shouted, "Fire!"

The crowd gasped as if one and then surged forward. Elizabeth was pressed against the railing as she was jostled to the side. She clung to it, desperate to keep her feet, and glanced down the stairs towards Mr. Darcy.

As everyone else plunged down the steps, pushing and yelling, Mr. Darcy met her gaze, and, to her astonishment, lowered his head and resumed climbing towards her. A man's flailing arm knocked Mr. Darcy's hat from his head, and Elizabeth watched, terribly frightened, as it tumbled end over end all the way to the floor below, where it was trampled under the feet of a panicked mob.

She shivered and looked back to the stairs. Surely Mr. Darcy must now bend to practicality and leave her to seek his own safety.

Instead, he continued to fight his way up the stairs.

To her. For her.

He gained a step, then leaned forward as though against a gale to take another. He had nearly reached Elizabeth, stretching forward over the remaining few steps, one arm extended to assist, when a dark-haired man flew past her, ramming his shoulder into Mr. Darcy's before slipping away into the fleeing horde.

Mr. Darcy, already a bit off-balance, was shoved to one side and backwards, his forward foot slipping up before him as he teetered precariously.

Elizabeth's world closed to anything not immediately before her. The steep marble stairs. The crowd, resembling a herd of wild horses. Mr. Darcy, attempting to regain his balance, arms waving, tipping backwards . . .

She gasped with horror and, releasing the rail, lunged forward.

As she did, the man who had collided with Mr. Darcy glanced back at him, and Elizabeth's heart hammered in her chest at the sight. He scowled, then melted away into the crowd.

One moment Darcy was reaching for Miss Elizabeth's hand, and the next, someone was shoving him backwards in a cowardly attempt to escape.

His world tilted.

In that instant, he saw it. He was going to fall down the stairs, and should the fall not kill him, he would be crushed beneath the feet of the frantic crowd.

There was a sharp tug at the back of his neck. Darcy's vision cleared enough to see that the slight Miss Elizabeth had taken hold of the front of his cravat, her entire body leaning backwards, her little silk slippers not affording her much purchase on the carpet. She slid forward a touch.

Once dragged onto the marble, her feet would fly out from beneath her and she would go down with him.

Their gazes met, hers determined and his, he was sure, resigned. Her fine eyes flashed with flame, and the pressure at the back of his neck intensified.

For one horrible moment, he was anchored only by the strength of his valet's knot and the stubbornness of one country miss. But it could not last.

The only thing worse than dying a humiliating death such as this would be harming Miss Elizabeth in a futile attempt to avoid it. "Let go!" he cried.

No sooner had he uttered the words than a tremendous blow at his back sent him flying in the opposite direction, up the remaining two stairs and directly towards her.

Miss Elizabeth tumbled backwards, unable to remove herself from his path, and he landed with all his weight atop her, his face in her . . . Oh, dear God.

She was beneath him, soft and warm, the dream of many nights flashing through his mind. It took but an instant to regain his bearings. His back was certainly bruised, but he had not fallen down the hard, steep stairs. He had not been flattened.

He was not dead.

But he *was* crushing the woman who was now lying still beneath him. Great God, he must be four stone heavier at the least.

Immediately, he shoved himself up on his forearms. He would have stood to help her up, but one of her hands was still caught in his cravat.

"There is no fire!" someone shouted. "No fire!" The message was called out from person to person as the crowd calmed.

Someone whistled behind Darcy, then another one guffawed. He ignored it.

"Miss Elizabeth," he said softly, gently removing her limp hand. "I am so very sorry. Are you injured?"

Her eyes were open, but she did not speak. Instead, she struggled for air, not unlike a fish caught on the line.

Suddenly, her breath returned with a dreadful rasp.

"My deepest apologies, madam," he said worriedly. He pushed himself up and sat back on his heels, unsure of what to do to assist her.

The first sound from her was a shaky laugh.

A laugh!

"Are you apologising for not falling to your death, Mr. Darcy?" she managed to say, still catching her breath. The shadow of a smile graced her countenance. "How extraordinary."

That faint twitch of her lips smote his heart.

Oh no.

This powerful sense of admiration he had been battling for months, ever since he had followed Bingley to town in the company of his sisters—it was not some foolish infatuation. It was not lust, though heaven knew he had experienced that. Worst of all, it was not going to recede.

Because it was love.

He was in love with Elizabeth Bennet.

Chapter Two

Darcy was aghast. All this time he had worked to put her out of his mind, and for at least the past month, he had congratulated himself on his success. What conceit to have prided himself on his discipline, for at the sight of one weak smile, it had all crumbled into dust. She did not know, she could not know, that he was intrigued by her. He had taken such pains to hide it! The last words he had spoken to her had been bitter ones about Wickham.

Yet Miss Elizabeth had still put herself in peril for him. Was there anywhere another woman like her?

"Darcy," he heard Fitzwilliam hiss in his ear. "For God's sake, man, stop staring. Stand up and help the woman to her feet. We must take our leave."

He complied immediately, offering Miss Elizabeth both hands to help her rise. A faint red blush coloured her cheeks as she took them. She glanced at Fitzwilliam, then at him, expecting, no doubt, to be introduced. There was a pause in the low chatter around them, and he imagined every person nearby straining their ears to hear her name.

Normally, he would not hesitate to complete the polite forms, but he had already heard a few impertinent remarks from the crowd. Better that none of those gossipmongers hear her name. Not until he could decide what to do.

"Thank you for your assistance, madam," he said very formally.

Miss Elizabeth frowned. "You are welcome, sir," she replied uncertainly.

"Niece," said a man who appeared suddenly at Miss Elizabeth's elbow. "Say farewell to your friends and let us depart."

The man was older than Darcy by perhaps ten years. He was neither as tall nor as broad, but he was handsome in a way that reminded him a little of Miss Bennet.

"But Uncle," Miss Elizabeth protested in a low voice, "I have something important to relate to Mr. Darcy."

This man was the tradesman, then.

Miss Elizabeth's uncle was fashionably but tastefully dressed. Clearly, he could afford a box at the theatre, and neither his speech nor his manners would have betrayed him as a man of business. Was this the deplorable connection Miss Bingley had bemoaned? A twinge of shame made Darcy shift uneasily from one foot to the other.

The man's eyes immediately took in the scene with what Darcy surmised was an unerring accuracy. "We must find our party," he said firmly to his niece.

Darcy was grateful. Miss Elizabeth did not seem to comprehend the delicate position they were in, but her uncle certainly did.

"Good evening, sir," Miss Elizabeth said with a shallow curtsy as she was led away.

Darcy purposely did not watch her depart. She was angry with him, but what was he to do? Did she expect him to bandy her family's name about where these cretins could hear? He had been lying fully atop her with her hand under his cravat and his face in her . . . Despite the unusual events that had made it necessary, terrible slanders would be flying about the theatre before those gathered about had even reached their carriages.

"Who said there was a fire?" he heard someone ask. "Dangerous, that!"

"Maybe it was Mr. Darcy, hoping to take advantage of the confusion," a woman snickered.

"Difficult to do," Fitzwilliam said warningly, "as the voice came from behind you and my cousin was on the stairs."

The woman lifted her brows and turned away.

"You ought to have chosen a darker corner for your dalliance, Darcy," said Mr. Carton, with whom Darcy had only a slight acquaintance.

A scattering of laughter met this declaration.

Darcy said nothing, only took a few steps in the man's direction. "Are you questioning my honour, sir?"

The vaguely amused expression disappeared. "Not at all." Carton glanced around. "Though I might be questioning hers." He darted off with a few of his friends before Darcy could issue a challenge.

A good thing, too. He deplored men who duelled.

"Come, Darcy," Fitzwilliam said, more urgently now. "We must remove ourselves."

Darcy nodded. By the time they had gained his carriage, he realised he had never learned the uncle's name, nor had he given the man one of his cards. How was he to assure that Miss Elizabeth suffered no ill effects from this evening? He could hardly knock on every door "somewhere near Cheapside," which was all the intelligence Miss Bingley had provided. The footman closed the door, and they made their way slowly out of the crowd of coaches.

Darcy did not recognise his cousin's growing agitation until Fitzwilliam threw his hat at him. He startled and then watched the hat fall to the floor.

"Darcy! Mind me! Who was that woman?"

"Miss Elizabeth Bennet," he replied.

"Bennet?" Fitzwilliam's countenance creased in thought. "Any relation to the MP from Shrewsbury?"

"What?" Darcy asked, distracted. "No, I do not believe so."

"Connected somehow to the Arlington line?"

"I doubt it."

Fitzwilliam pinched the bridge of his nose and took a deep breath. "Who was she, Darcy?"

"A woman I met when I visited Bingley in Hertfordshire last autumn."

"You met her in the country."

"Yes."

"This is worse than I thought. They will ferret it out and then imply that you planned to meet her here in London, away from her family."

"She was attending with her family. That was her uncle who took her away."

"Yet she was not with them when you knocked her over. Why was her hand in your cravat, man?"

"Miss Elizabeth kept me from falling. Did you not see her?"

"*I* kept you from falling, Darcy. Rather impressively, I must say."

"Had Miss Elizabeth not taken hold of my cravat to arrest my descent, you would not have reached me in time."

"I never saw her do it. I only heard you tell someone to release you." Fitzwilliam's brows lowered. "Of course, who can see anything over your enormous head?"

Darcy smiled a little. Trust his cousin to lighten the mood. "It is not my fault that Darcy men are made on a larger scale."

Fitzwilliam grinned back, but soon he grew sombre again, the light from the lanterns outside the windows casting an eerie shadow across his countenance. "Truly, Darcy, this may be a problem. You were wearing no hat, her hands were inside your clothing, and you did not precisely leap away. You were almost buried in her . . ."

"Stop, Cousin. You knocked me forward, and Miss Elizabeth could not remove herself from my path. It was an awkward fall, nothing more."

Fitzwilliam's laugh was almost a bark. "Awkward indeed. I should like to suffer such an accident one day."

"This is not that sort of situation, and I will not insult Miss Elizabeth by suggesting she had improper motives."

His cousin glanced out the window before he spoke again. "She said there was something of import to relate to you, before her uncle dragged her off. What do you think it was?"

"I mean to ask once I discover where her uncle lives."

Fitzwilliam threw his head back and stared at the ceiling of the coach. "You cannot be serious."

"She put herself at great risk to help me."

"And you thanked her."

"With words, not with actions. I am obliged to listen to whatever she has to say."

"And what if she asks you to marry her to save her reputation?"

I almost wish she would. The thought could not be spoken, but his cousin knew him all too well. Fitzwilliam's eyes narrowed.

"You like her."

Darcy shrugged. "I have tried not to."

"Has she any fortune or connections at all?"

He pursed his lips. Best to lay it all out at once. "Her father is a country squire, there are five unwed daughters, and the estate is entailed away to a distant, idiotic cousin."

"Portion?"

"I am certain it is negligible."

"That is a problem, Darcy." Fitzwilliam sat back.

Darcy shook his head slowly. "It gets worse."

"Please do not tell me she has a sister in the theatre," his cousin quipped.

"The heir to Longbourn is a parson who has the living at Hunsford."

"Lady Catherine's parson. Excellent," Fitzwilliam said, with a strangled laugh.

Darcy winced. "Furthermore, I helped Miss Bingley and Mrs. Hurst separate Bingley from Miss Elizabeth's eldest sister."

Fitzwilliam's frown was ferocious. "Why did you involve yourself in Bingley's concerns? Was she a fortune hunter?"

"No. Miss Bennet and Miss Elizabeth are ladies in every sense of the word. But the father is disinterested, and at every possible opportunity, the mother and younger sisters display a total want of propriety." Well, they might teach Miss Mary to be less pedantic. As for Mrs. Bennet and her youngest two daughters, he was uncertain anything could amend behaviour that had been left so long unchecked.

"So you would protect Bingley from such a connection, and yet you plan to contact her again yourself? Truly, what a woman to choose, Darcy!"

Darcy shook his head. "I did not choose her. I *cannot* choose her."

There was a pause as Fitzwilliam studied him as well as he could in the dim light of the coach. "But you would like to."

"It does not matter. I could not connect myself to such a family."

"But you would like to," Fitzwilliam repeated.

Darcy was silent.

"You *would*. You are considering throwing yourself away on this woman. I cannot believe it." There was no censure in his cousin's voice, only surprise.

"She is lovely, Fitzwilliam. Witty, kind. I have witnessed her deliver a set down without the victim even realising what had happened. I liked her last autumn and felt I might be in some danger. Therefore, I returned to London when Bingley's sisters closed Netherfield." He hesitated. "I have tried. I believed I had succeeded. But . . . she risked herself for me tonight."

Fitzwilliam said nothing in reply, just waited.

"I told her to release me," Darcy continued, "and her countenance . . . She was determined to keep me from falling, even if she was tossed down the stairs in consequence. I cannot be so ungentlemanly as to ignore her after that."

"She would be an incredibly fortunate woman to have you, Darcy," Fitzwilliam said at last. "But you must proceed cautiously. Make certain she is who you believe her to be, or your life will be a misery."

It might not come to that. He would not wish to offer to any woman simply because it was required of him. Still, Darcy nodded. He would think more on it tomorrow, when he was not so entirely done in.

"Elizabeth, you will accompany me to the study," her uncle said sternly as they handed over their coats to the maid.

Jane squeezed Elizabeth's hand and offered her a reassuring smile before turning towards the stairs.

The carriage ride back to Gracechurch Street had passed in absolute silence.

Elizabeth followed Uncle Gardiner into his study, and after a moment, her aunt slipped in behind them.

"Elizabeth," her uncle growled, "I need to know precisely what happened. All of it."

He had never been so severe with her in all her life, but she understood. She had relinquished the safety of her party to calm her racing thoughts, and in consequence, her uncle had not been present to protect her. Suddenly, she comprehended that if Mr. Darcy had not seen her there, he would not have been walking back up the steps when . . .

She related the entire story.

"So you say you took hold of his cravat to prevent his fall?" Uncle Gardiner shook his head solemnly. "He is a large man, Lizzy, and you are slight. You could not have saved him."

"You might, however, have been injured yourself," her aunt added.

"In the end, it was enough," she said. "I was able to hold on long enough for his friend to reach Mr. Darcy."

"Shoving him on top of you." He rubbed the back of his neck as he did whenever he suffered a headache.

"Yes." She stared at her feet. "That was unfortunate."

"We were following you out when Mr. Picton entered the box to greet us. I could not offend him by leaving to find you, and foolishly, I believed no trouble would find you in the hall."

"Or that you would return once you realised we were not with you," Aunt Gardiner said, gently admonishing her.

"Mr. Darcy said he would wait with me," Elizabeth admitted.

"What was it you intended to tell Mr. Darcy?" her uncle asked.

Elizabeth closed her eyes. "I can scarce believe it myself." She opened her eyes and met those of her aunt. "The man who pushed Mr. Darcy was Mr. Wickham. And I believe it was intentional."

Her aunt gasped. "Lizzy, we were speaking of Mr. Wickham only moments before the play ended. Perhaps he was merely on your mind. Are you entirely certain it was him?"

They had been speaking of Mr. Darcy, too, just before he materialized before her. Elizabeth pursed her lips before nodding. "I am certain, though I wish I was not. He turned to watch as he made his escape. It was brief, but I had a very exact view."

"That puts a rather different light on things," her uncle said grimly.

Aunt Gardiner nodded. "Mr. Darcy must be informed. Do you know his direction?" She looked at Elizabeth, who shook her head.

"He is a wealthy man from an old family," Uncle Gardiner replied. "I shall be able to find it."

"Uncle, Mr. Darcy has not been introduced to you. Why would he read your correspondence? He would be more likely to toss your note in the fire. We must go to see him."

"I thought you hated the man?" Aunt Gardiner inquired gently.

"I do not hate him."

Aunt Gardiner smiled a little. Uncle Gardiner's lips pinched, and his eyes narrowed.

"Very well. I have been vocal enough in my dislike for him, but surely, considering everything that has happened tonight, to continue in such a way would be foolish." She felt her cheeks warm. "And I confess that I already feel very, very foolish."

Her uncle grunted. "Merely stepping out into the hall before your party is a minor breach of propriety. It should not have resulted in such an outcome."

"Yet it has, and I have involved you and my aunt in what may yet disgrace me. I am so very sorry."

"Self-recrimination will do us little good now," said her aunt. "Let us instead bend our considerable talents to addressing the task before us."

"There is my sensible Margaret," Uncle Gardiner said fondly, before taking a deep breath. "Let us think on what is to be done. Lizzy, I must ask once more: You are completely certain that the man was Mr. Wickham?"

"I wish I could say that I was not," Elizabeth said. "Alas, I am."

"As unhappy as I am to think ill of anyone who hails from Derbyshire," her aunt said plainly, "there is no excuse for what he has done."

"Indeed," her uncle said. "It speaks of more than disappointment over a bequest."

"If indeed the story he told Lizzy was even true," Aunt Gardiner added.

That was a very good point. Mr. Wickham was the most handsome man she had ever met, and after being insulted by Mr. Darcy, it had been a balm to Elizabeth's wounded pride to be singled out by him. Now she wondered whether she had been chosen as his confidante not because she possessed any particular charm, but because Mr. Wickham had been sure that his poisonous words would fall in fallow ground.

How humiliating.

"He *was* very free with his grievances," her aunt said. "I ought to have warned you about that, Lizzy, but apparently, I am no less susceptible to a handsome face and a pretty manner than anyone else. You must not reproach yourself on that score."

"If her father was more interested in his daughters . . ." her uncle grumbled, but Aunt Gardiner hushed him.

"I will make certain your message is received by Mr. Darcy, Lizzy," her uncle said. "However, it is best that you depart with Sir William and Miss Lucas tomorrow. Although I believe you were not recognised, *I* may have been, and any alteration to your plans might be seen as suspicious."

"But you will go in person, Uncle?" Elizabeth hated to press him and indeed, Uncle Gardiner was not pleased by her insistence. But he nodded.

"I happen to agree with you, Elizabeth, this cannot be trusted to a servant. But you must leave this in my hands. Trust me to know how it is best to be done."

Elizabeth did trust her uncle, and she gave him to know as much.

He pressed her hand and offered her a small but genuine smile. "Goodnight then, Lizzy."

Aunt Gardiner kissed her lightly on the cheek. She was not normally so demonstrative, and this sign of support was gratefully received. Elizabeth squeezed her aunt's hand before making her way upstairs.

Chapter Three

Darcy's uncle, the earl, arrived the next morning before he had even finished his breakfast.

"What nonsense is this I hear about your behaviour at the theatre last night?" He tossed a newspaper down on the table. "Man cannot even sit to a meal without being lambasted about something or other," he muttered.

"Would you care to join me, Uncle?" Darcy asked drily.

"I would," the earl said, indicating to the footman to pour him some coffee. "Son of mine not awake yet?"

"He is on leave, Uncle. You know he stores up sleep during the months his regiment is in England."

The earl made himself a plate and Darcy, sure that his uncle wished to speak with him privately, nodded to the footmen, who closed the door on their way out.

"Fitzwilliam sent us a note last night about Miss Bennet."

"He said he would."

"He gave no other particulars, and the gossip in the paper quite shocked your aunt."

"As well it should, though I doubt there is much written that is true."

"Your aunt and I believe you should leave for Kent today. Take your sister and cousin with you."

"I am departing in a fortnight as it is, and Georgiana does not wish to accompany me."

"We can say you always meant to leave today, and Georgiana will travel with you. We would not have her exposed to the news being bandied about."

He need not ask what news that was. "I will not run away."

"It would be best were you not here when this lady's family comes to call."

Darcy's stomach soured. "How do you know they intend to call?"

"Why would they not? You gave them the perfect opportunity to demand a marriage, boy, taking her aside like that."

"Taking her aside?"

The earl handed Darcy the paper with the pertinent item on display. He scanned it. Scurrilous trash, as always. "I did not take her aside, as this says, nor were we hiding in the shadows." He sipped his coffee. "If we had been, no one would have seen us."

"That does not make it better, Darcy."

Darcy groaned wearily. "Uncle," he said, resigned, "someone yelled that there was a fire. In the confusion, a man running down the steps shoved me as he passed. The lady kept me from flying backwards. I am certain she saved me from a grave injury."

"A *lady* kept you from falling," his uncle said. "A great ox like yourself?" Scepticism dripped from each word.

He lifted his shoulders. "She prevented it long enough for Fitzwilliam to run into me from behind and send us both to the ground."

The earl grimaced. "Richard. Always a bludgeon when a fork would do." He sagged a little in his chair and then met his nephew's gaze. "So it is not true?"

"It is not."

"Then it is worse than I believed. The lady's family has a legitimate grievance." He rose to pour himself more coffee. "Do we know her?"

"You do not, but I am acquainted with her from my time with Bingley last autumn."

The earl set his cup down on the saucer with a clink, and Darcy only just kept from asking his uncle to mind the china. "You were in Hertfordshire last autumn."

"I was."

"Half a dozen significant estates there. I do not suppose she belongs to any of them?"

Darcy shook his head silently.

"Any relation to the MP? He would be an excellent ally. Little radical, but willing to go to great lengths to get things passed."

It was just like speaking with Fitzwilliam. "Doubtful."

"Well, then." The earl dipped a spoon into his shirred eggs. "You will not think of Anne?"

That was a subject that had not arisen in years. "No more now than the last time you inquired."

"Too bad. It would be a neat way out of this mess."

Lady Matlock stepped into the room followed by a footman. She was dressed for battle in a dramatic red day gown with intricate silver embroidery. "You would marry him off to Anne? That would be a rather permanent solution to a temporary problem."

If Darcy could only persuade his heart that Miss Elizabeth was a temporary infatuation! Leaving town while she resided here was likely for the best.

"Having you out of London should be enough for the gossip to die out." The earl waved at the footman, who filled a plate at the countess's direction and, once he had set it down at the table, was dismissed.

"Not nearly enough," his aunt said, pursing her lips at the earl. "You know this is my arena, dear. You concentrate on the Lords and leave the gossip to me." She addressed Darcy next. "It will become worse before it improves. Rosings is the better place for you just now."

"Very well," Darcy said. "I shall speak with my sister."

"I have been upstairs already," she informed him. "I thought having Georgiana readied to take a trip without delay was the best course of action." She waved off Darcy's resulting scowl. "Do not blame your servants. I told them your uncle would inform you."

Darcy glared at the earl, who shrugged. "Will you allow me time to put on my coat, or am I to be shoved in the carriage before I am properly dressed?"

His uncle raised his eyebrows. "That depends. How much longer do you intend to loll about?"

By ten o'clock, Darcy found himself rattling over the London streets in his carriage, Fitzwilliam sitting across from him. Georgiana, displaying a bit of the Darcy stubbornness herself, had begged him to remain at home, and he had complied. The earl and countess were forced to be satisfied with a word to her companion and a stern commandment to the servants that their niece should have no visitors but family until her brother's return.

"Georgiana was quite formidable." Fitzwilliam smiled. "It is good to see her recovering."

Darcy agreed. "Mrs. Annesley has been an excellent companion for her. She is more herself than she was, and her studies are proceeding well, but I cannot blame her for not wishing to accompany us. Her spirits are not yet high enough to withstand Lady Catherine."

Fitzwilliam huffed. "*My* spirits are barely adequate to the task."

Darcy chuckled.

"I thought I was back in Spain, being rousted from my bed in such a way."

"I believe this is all for naught. Miss Elizabeth is not the sort to insist on reparations."

"Ah, but her family may see things differently. Did you not say that her uncle is in trade?"

That was the problem, was it not? Her family. "That is what I understand, but he appeared as any other man of fashion last night. You saw him yourself."

"True," Fitzwilliam said, lifting the basket of food Darcy's cook had provided and beginning to rummage about inside it. "But he is still a tradesman. You must admit, you are a very tempting object for such a family. Despite the indignity of being tossed in the carriage without so much as a cup of coffee, I must agree with my mother and father. Best that you are not present to take his call should he attempt to make one."

Darcy rubbed at the bruise on his back before reclining into the squabs, watching as his cousin raided the basket. He mulled over Fitzwilliam's warning about Miss Elizabeth's family and then considered whether they were any different, in essentials, from his aunt Lady Catherine, who had long wished to see him marry her daughter. Arriving a fortnight early would give rise to his aunt's expectations in that quarter, expectations he had long denied. This change in their plans would necessitate delicate dissuasions, for he could not reveal his true reason for coming.

Journeying to Rosings might very well be a case of jumping out of the frying pan into the fire.

Elizabeth watched out of the window as the carriage rattled its way towards Kent. Sir William's conveyance was, like everything at Lucas Lodge, serviceable without being terribly comfortable. It was better than taking the post, which she and Maria would do on their way home, but that was all that could be said for it.

The other occupants of the carriage were asleep, a feat Elizabeth wondered at. Even were her back and neck not already sore from her collision with Mr. Darcy at the theatre last night, she would have found it difficult to rest when the coach's springs barely served their office. She watched out the window as the city gave way to the country, and then the green trees and long stretches of land still brown in the final weeks of winter stretched before them. She took a deep breath. It would be lovely here come the spring.

The Gardiners had been correct. She already felt as though the events of last night were receding into her distant memory. What was *not* receding was her newfound understanding of Mr. Wickham's character—and Mr. Darcy's. Unsettled, she had discussed it with her sister before they both fell asleep, and Jane had reminded Elizabeth that *she* had never believed Mr. Darcy so very bad.

One moment Elizabeth was gazing out at the landscape and dreaming of wildflowers, and the next, the coach lurched and listed. Maria slid down the bench and landed atop her, the girl's elbow striking sharply just below Elizabeth's ear. The carriage turned sharply and came to a stop partially across the road with the back of the box lifted slightly in the air.

Elizabeth tried to catch her breath as she clutched the back of the squabs to keep from pitching forward.

"Is everyone well?" she asked when Sir William did not.

He nodded, and Maria sniffled. "Yes," the girl said, weeping quietly. Elizabeth waited for Sir William to step out and check on his men, but when he remained where he was, she gently suggested that he ought.

"Quite right, Miss Elizabeth," he said, shaking himself out of his stupor. "Quite right, I thank you."

He stepped outside but did not turn back to assist her or Maria as Elizabeth had expected.

She closed her eyes briefly. Perhaps her character study of Sir William had not been unerring, but neither had it been entirely wrong. He was not a thoughtless man, only one better suited to routine than the unexpected.

"I think we ought to step down as well, Maria," Elizabeth informed the younger girl. The coach did not seem likely to turn over, but it was not stable, and remaining in the middle of the road in a disabled vehicle made her nervous. "Continue to hold on while I make my way out and then follow what I have done."

Slowly, Elizabeth edged across to the bench where Sir William had been sitting. Then, ever so carefully, she inched over to the door on the other side of the carriage, which still hung open.

When Elizabeth peered out, he was deep in conversation with his coachman. Not wishing to disturb them, she extended her leg as far as it would go, but without the steps, she still could not step directly onto the road. When she jumped down, her heel hit a part of the rut that had sent their poor conveyance to its doom, and her ankle turned outward.

Elizabeth yanked her foot up immediately and hopped on her good one. There was no immediate pain in her ankle, giving her hope that she was uninjured, but when she gingerly set her foot down again, the sharp twinge told her that it would likely swell.

"Are you hurt, Lizzy?" Maria asked sweetly from her precarious perch at the carriage door.

"A very little, Maria, nothing we must regard." Charlotte would set her to rights once they arrived. She held up her hand to help Maria, who took it and made her way down more easily.

Elizabeth tried to move her ankle a little, but the twinge did not recede. If she took very small, gentle steps, she could manage, but she would not be taking many walks in Kent, not for some days, at least.

Of all the rotten luck.

"Do you think we shall be stranded, Lizzy?" Maria asked plaintively. She twisted her hands and wrinkled her gloves.

"Your father is discussing plans with the coachman now." Elizabeth patted Maria's wrist. "We will not be here for long."

Elizabeth's assurance was, alas, premature. It had been nearly three-quarters of an hour by the time the horses were judged sound and the coachman rode ahead to Hunsford to seek help.

While they waited, Elizabeth entertained Maria with very minute descriptions of what the ladies had been wearing at the theatre the night before, though she did not mention how the evening had ended. Sir William contented himself with walking some way down the road to peer into the distance, then returning to them before beginning the circuit again.

After having walked back and forth several times, Sir William reached into the broken coach and withdrew several rugs, one of which he spread out on the ground at the side of the road on the far side of a tree. "Come, ladies," he said good-naturedly, "there is no need to stand about in the cold."

Elizabeth could not but agree. Her ankle was bothering her more now, and she thought she ought to put it up if she could. Sir William looked away while she and Maria arranged themselves on the rug, sitting together snugly to keep their clothing from touching the ground. Maria rolled up her shawl and handed it to Elizabeth to prop her foot upon, prompting her thanks. When they were ready, they called out and Sir William gallantly covered each of them with a rug of their own.

"Will you not be cold, Papa?" Maria inquired.

"My coat is quite warm," he replied, having regained his customary good humour. "It shall not be long now. Surely Johnson has reached Hunsford by now."

Elizabeth reached under the rug to check her watch. It had not been long; the coachman could not reach Hunsford so soon. The Collinses did not keep a carriage of their own, she was quite sure about that, so they would have to find a cart or some other way of transporting them all and their trunks to the parsonage once their messenger arrived. She sighed. It would be at least two hours before they might reasonably expect to be rescued.

They spent a quarter of an hour in relative silence before she heard the crunching sound of gravel under carriage wheels. Elizabeth glanced up to see a very fine black coach with a crest making its way in their direction. Sir William stood in the road and waved his arms to gain their attention. He continued longer than Elizabeth believed strictly necessary, for as the carriage approached the scene of their accident, the horses were already slowing.

At first, the coachman remained atop the carriage and only a large footman stepped to the front to speak with Sir William. Elizabeth supposed it was the safe thing to do, but really, Sir William could not appear any less threatening. She and Maria stood, rolled up the rugs, and arranged their skirts.

The footman called out, then the carriage rocked a bit to one side and a gentleman emerged. She knew this only because she could see part of a top hat bobbing above the back of the horse, but when the man came into view, Elizabeth's mouth dropped open.

This could not be happening to her.

"Mr. Darcy!" cried Sir William. "Well met!"

Chapter Four

Darcy climbed out of the coach to offer his assistance to the unfortunate travellers, but he soon wished he had not. For there was Sir William Lucas of Lucas Lodge, standing beside a carriage whose front axle had splintered and given way, the front of the box pointing to the centre of the road.

The bluff man called out his name in a relieved greeting, and Darcy gave him a hurried bow.

"Sir William. Are you and your party well?"

"Indeed we are, sir, indeed we are. My coachman has gone for help, but if we might presume, the ladies have been out in the cool air for some time."

Darcy vaguely recalled that there were two Lucas daughters, the elder a plain but sensible woman not much younger than he, and the younger closer to Georgiana's age. "Of course. They may wait in my carriage while we make arrangements. Where are you headed?" If their journey was taking them the same way, he would invite the Lucas family to join him. If not, they would have to turn back to Bromley, as it was the nearest posting inn.

"To the Hunsford parsonage, sir," Sir William said proudly. "My eldest daughter is lately married to the Reverend Mr. Collins."

It took Darcy but a moment to work out that if Miss Charlotte Lucas was now Mrs. Collins, and Mrs. Collins lived in Kent, then there was one lady in Sir William's party who was unaccounted for.

His gaze moved to the women standing with the rugs they had been using to keep warm. One of them was the young Miss Lucas, but the other . . .

"This is not happening," he muttered, running his hand down his face.

"What is not happening?" Fitzwilliam asked from beside him.

Darcy sighed, shook his head, and motioned at Sir William's back. The older man had gone to escort the women to the carriage. His carriage. Where he was riding. "That," he said, inclining his head in Sir William's direction.

Fitzwilliam glanced at him. "I say, Darcy, are you unwell?"

"I know Sir William from Hertfordshire," Darcy said flatly, ignoring Fitzwilliam's question. Yes, he was unwell, though it was no common ailment that afflicted him.

"I say, that is a coincidence."

"Not as much a coincidence as who is riding with him."

Fitzwilliam finally caught on. "Do you mean . . .?"

Darcy nodded. "She could have no idea I was coming into Kent today."

"She must have learned of it somehow."

"How? I did not know myself until a quarter of an hour before your parents sent us off. Are you suggesting she has spies in an earl's home?"

Fitzwilliam rubbed the back of his neck, chagrined. "No, of course not."

Darcy watched as Sir William offered his arm to each of the ladies and made his way very slowly forward. Why were they moving at such a pace? Miss Elizabeth had clearly identified him, as she refused to look up. But she was taking infinitesimally small steps as they all moved forward. He studied her progress, and his heart contracted painfully. She was injured. Was it from him landing atop her last night or from suffering this accident today?

Her past hours had been worse than his.

"Allow me, Darcy," Fitzwilliam said quietly. "If she wishes to swoon into someone's arms, they should not be yours." He strode off. Darcy heard his cousin introducing himself and watched him make a dashing bow. But Miss Elizabeth refused to take his arm. Her voice rang out across the air. He wondered whether Fitzwilliam could hear the slight tremor in it.

"I thank you, but I do not require your assistance, Colonel. I am capable of walking to the carriage with Sir William's help."

"Madam," Fitzwilliam began, but she interrupted, her tone gentler now.

"Forgive me," she said, softer now, "but I do not know you, sir."

"We have just been introduced. And you know Darcy, certainly."

One of Miss Elizabeth's eyebrows arched challengingly. "We have met. However, I would not presume on such a brief acquaintance as ours."

It was entirely prudent of her to say as much, given their predicament. Darcy did not understand why her rebuff hurt.

Miss Elizabeth's brusque manners clearly surprised Sir William and his daughter, but they said nothing.

By the time Fitzwilliam relented, the entire group had moved close enough to Darcy that he could make his own bow. "Miss Lucas, Miss Elizabeth."

Miss Lucas dipped her head and offered him a curtsy that was nearly deep enough for royalty, but Miss Elizabeth merely stared at him with a mocking smile. "Good day, Mr. Darcy. I must thank you for the use of your coach."

"My pleasure, Miss Elizabeth." It was not his pleasure. His pleasure would be to ask to call on her. "Anders is the best coachman in London. You will be in good hands."

When he said nothing more, Miss Elizabeth turned to hobble over to the steps. As she moved away, Darcy saw a bit of colour on one side of her face, just above her jawline, and his guilty conscience overrode his sense of caution. He stepped around her, and when she stopped, he took her chin in one hand, gently turning her head to one side to better view the bruise. "The ankle is not your only injury."

He nearly asked whether the bruise was a result of their fall last night, but Miss Elizabeth was discreet. He had not seen the Lucases at the theatre, and therefore there was every possibility that they did not know what had happened.

"I fell on Lizzy when the carriage tipped," Miss Lucas said anxiously. "Oh, Lizzy, you never said a word!"

"There was no need, Maria, I am quite well," Miss Elizabeth replied, narrowing her eyes at him. He felt the shock of her gaze and swallowed. Her cheeks pinked. "If you please, sir?"

He was still holding her chin. Embarrassed, he dropped his hand.

Miss Lucas entered the carriage first. Miss Elizabeth ought to have climbed in after. Instead, she bit her lip and took the footman's hand, putting her injured foot on the bottom step with a bit of a wince as she pushed up. Darcy waited for Sir William to assist her, but he seemed to be looking at them rather than at her.

Miss Elizabeth squared her little shoulders and lifted her foot again.

This was torture.

Darcy grabbed her unceremoniously with both hands around her waist and lifted her inside. "Miss Lucas," he said authoritatively, "have Miss Elizabeth put her leg up on the bench."

"We will manage very well, Mr. Darcy," Miss Elizabeth replied pertly. "If you would be so kind as to close the door."

The footman complied.

Fitzwilliam took him by the arm and dragged him away. "What in blazes are you about, Darcy?" he hissed. "You touched her face *and* her waist. Are you *wishing* to land yourself in the parson's mousetrap?"

"She was in pain. She might have done more damage to herself."

"Which she is old enough and presumably wise enough to know. You have no responsibility to see to her care. That is the old man's business."

"Sir William," Darcy ground out, keeping his voice low, "is a good sort of man, Fitzwilliam, but he is not accustomed to the world outside his hamlet. I can promise you he is not up to the task of escorting an obstinate woman like Miss Elizabeth."

Fitzwilliam surveyed the coach and then turned back to Darcy. "Who is?" he asked slyly, straightening. "Might it be you?"

"No," Darcy said, closing his eyes. *Yes.* "But I cannot see any way around it—they must have the carriage, Fitzwilliam, and we cannot go into Kent with them."

"Indeed not. It is bad enough they will be seen to arrive in your coach. The Darcy crest is well known near Rosings."

"What else can I do?"

Fitzwilliam tipped his head to one side. "Are you sure you wish to continue distancing yourself? At least she is pretty, Darcy, and she has some fire in her."

"Fitzwilliam," Darcy growled warningly.

"Very well. I must say, I am feeling quite charitable since Miss Bennet's presence shall spare us a lengthy exile in Kent. Shall we see your friends off and ride back to London, or shall you pass town and keep on until you reach Pemberley?"

Darcy glared at his unrepentant cousin.

"You must admit, Darcy," Fitzwilliam said with a little laugh, "either she is the best fortune hunter you or I have ever encountered, or . . ."

"Or what?"

"Or fate has taken a hand."

"I do not believe in fate."

"That is just the thing," Fitzwilliam replied. "You do not have to."

Elizabeth sat on the generously padded bench with an ungracious huff and immediately regretted it when a sharp pain shot up her leg. Her quick intake of air alerted Maria, who helped settle her properly and draped a rug over her for modesty.

How dare that man touch her? Twice? How could he be so lost to their situation?

While Maria fussed, Elizabeth's anger cooled. While touching her in any manner had been unwise, Mr. Darcy *had* been concerned for her. She had always believed him perfectly indifferent, but she had read the guilt in his eyes.

This revelation must now be added to those she had been gathering since the theatre. Mr. Darcy had been gentlemanly, even chivalrous, and he had certainly been brave. His impatience with her a moment ago had only been a result of thinking he had hurt her.

She laughed quietly, a little snuffling laugh, and dropped her face in one hand. She had no such excuse. Only that when he had touched her, her skin had heated in a rush and her mind had gone blank. How mortifying to discover in less than a day that Mr. Darcy was not anything like she had thought only a few days before. Aunt Gardiner had always said that a man could be best known by how he reacted in a crisis. By that measure—despite his forwardness with her just now—Darcy was a very good man indeed.

Uncle Gardiner had insisted she separate herself from town and the rumours. Sound advice had not Mr. Darcy had precisely the same idea! Whoever could have predicted that he would travel south, into Kent, and not north to his estate?

As more rational thought returned to her, Elizabeth suddenly sat up. This was her chance to warn Mr. Darcy! She had nearly forgotten about it once her uncle promised to deliver her message. But he could not fulfil that promise, as Mr. Darcy was no longer in London!

The door to the coach opened, and Sir William climbed in. "Very impressive gentlemen, I must say. They have offered us the Darcy carriage to take us all the way to the parsonage."

"Will they not be joining us, Father?" Maria inquired.

A more pertinent question Elizabeth could not have asked herself.

"No, they will ride," Sir William said.

"What is their destination?" Elizabeth asked as politely as her sudden sense of urgency would allow.

Sir William was stuck by her question. "I did not ask, Miss Elizabeth, so I am afraid I do not know."

Elizabeth tried to smile, but she could not feel sanguine. She had allowed her confusion and a little pain to impede the delivery of vital news. Perhaps the gentlemen were also headed for Hunsford. Would they not be, if for no other reason than to retrieve the carriage? She heard the clip-clop of horse hooves and turned to look outside.

Mr. Darcy and Colonel Fitzwilliam were indeed on their horses, but they were headed in the opposite direction, back towards London.

Were Elizabeth not a lady, this would have been the perfect moment for a heartfelt curse.

Elizabeth enjoyed travelling, but she had never before considered how much pleasanter it could be when one had the funds for such a splendid conveyance as Mr. Darcy's carriage. Compared to Sir William's coach, it was like riding on air.

"It was very gentlemanly of Mr. Darcy," Sir William said, not for the first time. "Very good of him indeed."

Maria could only agree, and Elizabeth nodded along. As they left the high road and turned into the lane, she was grateful to approach the parsonage at last. They rode alongside the paling, which must be the boundary to Rosings Park. At last, after a very trying evening and morning, they stopped at a small gate at the end of a short gravel path to the house.

She alighted with care and was welcomed with such affection by Charlotte that she could not repine accepting the invitation. Her cousin's behaviour was no different now than it had been last autumn, and he kept them some minutes standing at the gate while he made minute inquiries into the health of her family.

"Elizabeth," Charlotte whispered to her, "whose carriage is this?"

Charlotte was a discreet creature. Alas, her father was not.

"Mr. Darcy's carriage?" Mr. Collins exclaimed from where the two men were in conference. "But where is the gentleman? I must offer him my greatest thanks and solicitude for rendering such aid to all my dear family. Such graciousness, such condescension!"

Chapter Five

Charlotte gave Elizabeth a sly look. "My father's coachman arrived only a short time before you. We were searching for a cart to fetch you all when you arrived." She leaned over to whisper, "I always thought Mr. Darcy liked you, Eliza. Promise that we shall speak of it soon."

Mr. Darcy had certainly *not* liked her, but Elizabeth agreed. With both Sir William and Mr. Collins together, it was unlikely anyone else would be able to speak for some time.

When Maria recalled Elizabeth's ankle, she hurried over to her sister, who then reproved her friend. "Allow me to assist you to the house. You really ought to have said something before."

How she could have broken into Mr. Collins's prepared welcome without appearing insufferably rude, Elizabeth did not know—and she had no desire to begin what she feared might be an awkward visit in such a way. Better to allow Mr. Collins to have his stage. Her injuries were trifling. A day or two would see her again in the best of health.

Suspecting that Charlotte would also appreciate some time alone with her, Elizabeth was more than willing to acquiesce. It would be lovely to sit in her bedchamber and have a serious conversation. For all her friend appeared to be content, Elizabeth had worried for her.

When they had made their excuses to the gentlemen, Charlotte helped Elizabeth to her chamber and then left briefly to take Maria to hers. Upon returning, she helped Elizabeth remove her stocking and shook her head. "You ought to have bound this up before, Eliza."

"With what?" Elizabeth asked, her cheer a little forced. "Your father was there. I could hardly rip up my petticoats. Not to mention it might scandalise your sister."

"Maria is still young," Charlotte said fondly, as she laid out everything she required and then set to work. She did not possess the same gentle touch as Jane, but she was careful and efficient. Elizabeth had to admit that she ought to have done something more about the ankle, for binding it now was a more painful business than it would have been had she felt at liberty to tend to it sooner.

Charlotte glanced over at the door that was still firmly shut and sat down on the side of the bed. "Now Eliza, I must know. How is it you all arrived in Mr. Darcy's coach? I would not have recognized the crest, for I believe they used Mr. Bingley's carriage when he resided at Netherfield." She said nothing further about Mr. Bingley.

Elizabeth appreciated her friend's delicacy. Her letters to Charlotte had not mentioned the Bingleys, for it seemed clear all hope was at an end there.

"By some terrible twist of fate, they were travelling behind us," Elizabeth said with a little sigh.

"Rather fortunate twist, I would say. Why should it be terrible?"

"Because I never wished to see him again," Elizabeth said lightly.

Charlotte tutted. "You must admit, he paid you a good deal of attention when he was in Hertfordshire. He did ask you to dance at the ball."

"I still cannot fathom why, when he found me so lacking at the assembly." There was no heat in the declaration, not anymore. Only curiosity.

"Perhaps he changed his mind," Charlotte said teasingly.

"How could he when he is never wrong?"

Charlotte shook her head fondly at Elizabeth. "By the time of the ball, Mr. Darcy did not seem to dislike you. And while any gentleman might have allowed you to take shelter in his carriage while the men made arrangements, they would not have sent you off in it." She met Elizabeth's eye. "Mr. Darcy's willingness to do so speaks to his feelings, my dear."

"He is a more gentlemanly man than I first believed," Elizabeth confessed. "But it does not follow that his interest tends that way. And even if you *are* correct," she said, lifting her hand to cut off Charlotte's protest, "that is no proof he would ever stoop to make an offer of marriage to a woman like me."

"You are a gentleman's daughter, Eliza."

"And he is a gentleman; so far we are equal," Elizabeth teased. "Indeed, I feel my own worth perhaps too much."

They both laughed softly.

"But you know as well as I that my father's wealth is a fraction of Mr. Darcy's, and I daresay there would be many obstacles to such a match."

"Would you wish for him to ask you, Eliza?"

She shook her head decisively. "No."

"Are you sure?"

Elizabeth seriously considered Charlotte's question. She must, for if her trip into Kent was not enough to stop any gossip there might be in London, it might be a decision she was required to make.

Or would she?

Mr. Darcy would never request her hand. If it came to it, he might offer her family a settlement of some sort to make the entire incident go away, but he would not take so irrevocable a step. "I am sure," she said.

"Well then," Charlotte said briskly, "Lady Catherine will be mightily relieved, as she has her heart set on Mr. Darcy offering for her daughter."

Elizabeth shook her head. She was forgetting everything important today. "Is that not already decided?" Mr. Wickham's assurances were not to be trusted, but Mr. Collins had made the claim as well.

"It is by Lady Catherine."

"And by your husband."

"Who has his information from his patroness," Charlotte replied. "Miss de Bourgh is a frail, sickly woman who rarely speaks in company. I do not think she ought to marry at all. However, no one is likely to consult *me* on the matter." She stood. "You should remain here until dinner. Maria and I shall help you down. Unless you would prefer a tray be brought up?"

This was a kind offer indeed, for the parsonage could not have so many servants that one might easily be spared to wait upon her alone. "Not at all, Charlotte. I shall be perfectly well by dinnertime, I am quite sure."

Darcy dragged himself up the stairs to his chambers where a hot bath was being drawn. His mind was whirling with thoughts of Miss Elizabeth. She had been so cool, so proper. Was she angry he had not arranged to speak with her uncle? He could not blame her if she were. Still, when it came to Miss Elizabeth, he could never be sure. It was just as likely she did *not* expect him to make an offer and was trying to protect her reputation in whatever way was available to her.

His desire and his duty had never been so at odds. What good was duty when it harmed a woman who least deserved it?

Did Miss Elizabeth presume he was a cad? His uncle would suggest he arrange a settlement for her should circumstances require it, but was that enough for her? Was it enough for *him*?

Just as Darcy was about to remove his cravat, Hoskins knocked on the door.

"Enter."

"Sir," his valet said as he entered, "there is a man from Picton's asking to speak with you. Says it is urgent."

Darcy stared at the man. "What could be so urgent about the coal order, Mr. Hoskins?"

"I am sure I do not know, sir, but apparently, he was most insistent. He told the footman he is here on your behalf and will not leave until he meets with you."

He might just have the man removed, but Darcy did not wish to have any further commotion about the house. "Ask Colonel Fitzwilliam to join me downstairs, Mr. Hoskins."

"Sir." Hoskins inclined his head and exited the room.

He surveyed his apparel. Dusty and smelling of horse. Well, whoever had insisted upon seeing him right away would have to take Darcy as he was.

When he reached the servant's entrance, Darcy came to a sudden halt. For there, in workman's clothing—no, his apparel was finer than that, though only just—stood the man whom Miss Elizabeth called uncle.

He certainly did *not* work for Picton's.

Darcy ordered the footman who was waiting for his arrival to leave and keep the hall clear. Miss Elizabeth's family had come to call after all, and how ingeniously! He fought against a sharp sting of disappointment.

"Do not look at me like that, Mr. Darcy," the other man said with a glower, taking a single step inside. "I took a hackney here in an attempt to reach you earlier in the day without being recognized, but your knocker was down. I was forced to proceed by other means." He muttered something to himself that sounded like "my wife's idea."

"I was not in town earlier in the day," Darcy said sternly. "My return was unexpected."

The man's expression softened a bit. "I suppose that is better than hiding inside and refusing to answer your door, though by all rights you ought to have been waiting for my call."

Darcy was affronted, but the man briefly squeezed his eyes shut, then opened them and said, "My apologies, Mr. Darcy. I am not accustomed to disguise, and this entire situation sits ill with me. However, I made a promise to my niece. I have sent her to Kent . . ."

"I know."

"I beg your pardon?"

Darcy shook his head, still annoyed at the man's insult to his honour. "What have you to tell me, sir?"

The man's eyes narrowed. "Lizzy wished to come herself, but my wife and I judged it best that she depart as planned."

"She was always meant to journey to Kent today?"

"Of course. She travelled here with the Lucases. We attended the theatre as a treat for her since she was only to be with us overnight."

Darcy felt his heart lift. Miss Elizabeth had always planned to visit her friend. He had not driven her from town, nor had she attempted to put herself in his way.

"You have distracted me from my purpose," Miss Elizabeth's uncle said with some asperity.

"What purpose would that be?" Fitzwilliam inquired boldly, striding into the room.

Their visitor eyed Fitzwilliam and then turned his gaze to Darcy, who nodded. "That you be made aware who it was that attempted to toss Mr. Darcy down the stairs last night."

Darcy felt as though someone had doused him with icy water. "What did you say?"

"Who are you?" Fitzwilliam demanded.

"Mr. Edward Gardiner," he said with a slight lift of his lips that was both gently teasing and a little mocking. "Silver and stationery, silks and scents." He doffed his hat and offered them a shallow bow. "Now, may I relay my message and release us all from this uncomfortable conference?"

Had Mr. Gardiner nothing else to say? No other demands to make?

"Lizzy wished me to say that last night it was Mr. Wickham who deliberately tried to shove you down the stairs."

"Wickham is in Hertfordshire," Darcy said without thinking.

Fitzwilliam's eyes shot to Darcy's. "*Is* he?"

Mr. Gardiner frowned. "I am aware he has been there all autumn, but he was at the theatre last night. Elizabeth was completely certain."

Fitzwilliam's expression darkened.

Darcy met Mr. Gardiner's eye. "This is all you took such pains to say?"

"This is all."

"You went to such lengths . . ."

"To warn you. Yes."

"Why?" Fitzwilliam was not asking but demanding an answer.

Mr. Gardiner was incredulous and not a little offended. "Do you think us so deficient in morals or feelings, sir? Mr. Darcy's health, perhaps his very life, may be at risk. It is only right to put him on his guard, and, had the incident at the theatre last night not required discretion, I should have sent a note the moment my niece informed me. Things being as they are, Elizabeth won my promise that I should relay this information in person. Discreetly."

Darcy could not comprehend it. They might have left him in his ignorance and been safer from the wagging tongues of the ton. He would never have known.

"You came with the coal," he said, perplexed.

"Mr. Picton is a friend who witnessed much of the incident. He told his men I had business here. And now that I have completed it, I shall leave with them and go home."

Darcy stood straighter and held the man's gaze. "May I know where that is, Mr. Gardiner?"

Mr. Gardiner reached into his coat and held out a card.

"Very good," Darcy said, taking it. "I thank you."

Mr. Gardiner inclined his head. "Good evening, gentlemen."

"Good evening, Mr. Gardiner."

As Darcy watched, Mr. Gardiner exited the servants' entrance and bounded up the stairs to the street, where the coal cart awaited him. He easily hopped up onto the back of the wagon, then pulled his hat forward over his eyes and cast his head down. Even were the most determined wags watching the townhouse, they would never associate this coal worker with the elegant man who had hurried Miss Elizabeth from the theatre last night.

Darcy closed the door.

Fitzwilliam turned to Darcy, a quizzical expression on his face. "He did not insist you make his niece an offer."

"No."

"I rather like this Mr. Gardiner," Fitzwilliam said. It was a great compliment, for while Fitzwilliam made himself liked everywhere he went, he rarely extended his own approval.

Darcy nodded. "So do I."

"Now," said Fitzwilliam, blue eyes turning steely as he transformed from Darcy's cousin into the colonel, "what are your plans for Wickham? For I should dearly like to meet with him again."

Darcy ran a hand through his hair, only then recalling how dusty he was. "Baths first, if they have not gone cold," he said. "Then dinner."

"And *then* we plan?"

"And then we plan."

Chapter Six

Elizabeth's ankle was somewhat improved when she woke near dinnertime, and Charlotte's arm was all she required to make her way gently downstairs to the dining room.

Sir William sat next to Mr. Collins with Maria on her father's other side. Elizabeth sat across from Maria, closer to Charlotte, who took the mistress's chair. Fortunately, the table was small enough not to make the grouping awkward, and the conversation was warm and easy. Even over dessert, when Mr. Collins dominated the discussion with an explanation of his garden as well as his hopes for honey and beeswax from his hives, it was not unpleasant.

Just as Elizabeth had determined that she could tolerate Mr. Collins well enough to enjoy the weeks of her visit here, there was the sound of a carriage in the drive.

Charlotte and Mr. Collins exchanged baffled looks.

"Who could that be?" Charlotte wondered.

Elizabeth understood from Mr. Collins that Lady Catherine often sent them home from Rosings in one of her carriages, but he had said nothing of them being retrieved by one. A strident voice rang out from the hall, startling her.

"Where is she?"

"Where is who?" Maria whispered, her complexion paling.

Mr. Collins's chair nearly toppled as he leapt to his feet and hurried away. "My lady!" he exclaimed, racing from the room. His voice floated back to them. "I cannot tell you what an honour it is to have you condescend to visit my humble abode!"

Charlotte frowned and pushed her own chair back in a far more deliberate manner. "I cannot understand why she should be here now, interrupting our meal. She would never deign to sit with us."

Elizabeth was just as bemused. "I expect we will soon discover her purpose."

"I do not believe we can escape it. She is a very attentive neighbour." Charlotte said low enough that only Elizabeth could hear. She placed her napkin on the table and stood.

The voice, which Elizabeth now knew belonged to none other than the highly extolled Lady Catherine de Bourgh, spoke again, though given its strength, it might better be described as a bellow. "Where is she? Where is this viper you have brought into our midst?"

Both Sir William and Maria's eyes widened almost comically as Mr. Collins began to apologise, although it was clear from the vague statements flowing forth from his mouth that he had no idea for what he was begging pardon.

Elizabeth glanced at Charlotte. Would her husband ever offer her the protection her friend deserved from this belligerent woman?

The grande dame herself soon appeared in the doorway, her appearance everything elegant and refined. At least it would have been, a generation past. Heeled shoes made her appear taller than she was, and a white wig was perched somewhat precariously upon her head.

Lady Catherine wore panniers under her brocade gown, which made it difficult for her to pass through the small entry, and rather than turn a little to the side, she stopped there, trapping Mr. Collins behind her as her wig slid ever so slightly to one side. Elizabeth wished devoutly for a sudden breeze to unsettle it further still. The woman deserved it for so rudely interrupting their meal.

Sir William began to stand, but sat again, then reversed course, unsure of what to do as Lady Catherine had not actually entered the room. Mr. Collins's head rose and fell as he bobbed first to one side of Lady Catherine and then the other in an attempt to see around her. Lady Catherine paid neither man any mind, coolly assessing first Maria and then Elizabeth.

"You!" she cried, pointing a long, bejewelled finger at Elizabeth. "You will leave this house at once and return to whatever hovel in the country from whence you have come."

"Excuse me?" Elizabeth asked, shocked. All she had done was walk up the stairs and sleep the afternoon away. She could not possibly have done anything that might offend Lady Catherine.

"You arrived in my nephew's carriage?"

"I did, as did Sir William and Miss Lucas." She wished to be perfectly clear that she had not been in Mr. Darcy's carriage alone.

"You met with my nephews at the theatre last night?"

How could she possibly know? Elizabeth supposed there was little point in denying it. "I did."

Lady Catherine was unmoved. "Then you are she. If you were sensible of your honour and his, you would not seek to leave the sphere in which you were raised!"

"Lady Catherine, I am afraid I do not understand."

The lady was incensed. "We have not been introduced!"

"Forgive me, madam," Elizabeth replied tartly. "As you have arrived without invitation and interrupted my repast to shout at me, I believed us beyond social niceties."

"You will not speak to me!" Lady Catherine cried out before recalling herself and lowering her voice. "But you *will* leave Rosings. And now."

"You expect me to leave?" Elizabeth cried. "By what means, madam?"

The great lady had apparently given up the pretence of ignoring her. "That is your own concern."

"It is indeed, and I shall not do it." Elizabeth saw, to her dismay, that Charlotte's shoulders had slumped.

Elizabeth had never been so glad to have refused Mr. Collins's proposals. She and Lady Catherine would have been on a field of honour, duelling with their parasols, before the first month of their acquaintance was complete. She would have laughed at the notion had everyone else in the room not been too stunned to laugh with her.

"I shall see her off myself, Lady Catherine," her bumbling cousin said, among a great many other things. "I do not know in what way my cousin has offended you, but I can only say I am very sorry for it. I am sure that when she realises what it is that she has done, she will be very sorry, too."

"Well," Lady Catherine said, mollified. "Have your maid gather her things."

If Mr. Collins would not take her side, she would have to do so for herself. "Lady Catherine, I am not leaving in the dark. If my family cannot host me for our visit, I shall depart in the morning."

"Mr. Collins has ordered you out. Stubborn, headstrong girl! Can you truly have the audacity to inform Mr. Collins what you will and will not do in his house?

The irony of the statement was not lost on Elizabeth, but there was nothing to be gained by pointing it out. "Mr. Collins has only spoken to you, madam. He has *not* ordered me out, nor would any man of God send his own cousin out into the dark on her own. Anything that might befall me would then be on his head," she said pointedly, "and my father would certainly insist upon a satisfactory explanation."

Mr. Collins was becoming so red in the face, Elizabeth thought he might fall over.

"Perhaps . . ." Mr. Collins said, but was cut off.

"I *have* the explanation, you impertinent girl!" Lady Catherine said imperiously. "You are the jezebel who has thrown herself at *my* nephew, Mr. Darcy! I know it all! My brother sent me word express that my nephews would come to me to avoid a scandal, and Darcy's own servants relayed the rest!"

The coachman and the footmen. They had likely taken Mr. Darcy to the theatre and picked him up. They might have heard a great deal as they waited in line, and they had all witnessed his solicitousness this morning.

Lady Catherine stopped to catch her breath before beginning again. "You would have the gall to wish an invitation into my home for tea, to sit with my daughter whom you intend to displace as Mrs. Darcy. It is not to be borne. It shall not be."

Elizabeth arched one brow. "Lady Catherine, I feel I must point out that I have never requested such an invitation."

"You will leave this house at once!" Lady Catherine commanded.

The astonishment of those gathered about the table was extreme. Elizabeth prepared to speak again, but felt a hand drop lightly over her own and glanced at Charlotte.

"Lady Catherine," her friend said quietly. "You forget yourself. This house is not Rosings, it is the parsonage, and it is not for you to dismiss my guests." She cast an unhappy look at Elizabeth. "If Elizabeth must return home, she will do so in the morning, when we can see to her safety and comfort."

The older woman drew herself up to a not inconsiderable height. "I shall remember this ingratitude, Mrs. Collins."

"Oh!" cried Mr. Collins, but nothing else. His hand flew to his mouth.

"It is not ingratitude, Lady Catherine," Charlotte said mildly. "I have no desire to offend. However, it is my duty as Miss Bennet's hostess and my honour as her friend to ensure her well-being. As mistress of such a large and prosperous estate yourself, you understand that such duties cannot be neglected."

Mr. Collins gurgled quite loudly.

Lady Catherine's face puckered as though she had partaken of something very sour. "And this is how you repay my notice of you, Mrs. Collins? Very well. I take no leave of you, for you deserve no such notice." Her eyes narrowed until Elizabeth wondered whether the older woman could even see. "I am greatly displeased."

Upon that pronouncement, Lady Catherine swept out of the room and the house without another word, Mr. Collins scurrying after her, begging her not to go.

"Oh dear," Sir William said, probably because he could think of nothing else to say. Maria's mouth hung open, and Elizabeth was sorry for having exposed the girl to such a violent argument. But she could not have done any differently. What sort of woman was Lady Catherine, to insist upon throwing Elizabeth out into the night?

They all remained in silence until the carriage could be heard leaving. Mr. Collins did not return.

Elizabeth shook herself and grasped her friend's hand. "Charlotte, I must apologise to you, for I had no notion that my presence would create such grief. If I have been the cause of any argument between you and your husband, I can only offer . . ."

"No, Eliza," Charlotte said firmly, though she was a little pale, "you have in fact done me a great service. Mr. Collins depends far too much upon Lady Catherine's good opinion. I try to be a good wife and placate her, but the fact is that she has only the one living to offer, and she cannot turn us out of this one."

"What does that mean?" Maria asked timidly.

"It means," Charlotte explained to her younger sister, "that only Mr. Collins's bishop can remove him from this parish, and then only if he were to engage in illegal or immoral acts that made him unsuited for his role. I would have preferred to keep the peace, but all we have truly lost in this is Lady Catherine's unwanted advice on how to run my house and a few uncomfortable dinners or teas."

"And perhaps," Elizabeth said, "when divided from Lady Catherine's particular condescension, your husband will learn to value his wife's opinion above that of Lady Catherine's?"

"That would be an excellent consequence," Charlotte agreed. Then she smiled at her father and sister before returning her attention to Elizabeth. "But now you must tell us what happened between you and Mr. Darcy, Eliza. I thought you had not seen him since Mr. Bingley's party left Netherfield last November?"

"I had not, but we met one another at the theatre last night, that much is true," Elizabeth said with a sigh. Lady Catherine had truly let the cat out of the bag. Even if Charlotte's servants did not relate the story far and wide, the servants at Rosings certainly would. All she could do was limit, temporarily, how much of it could be sent back to Hertfordshire.

Alas, with the Lucas family now connecting Meryton and Hunsford, full disclosure could not be long.

"How extraordinary," Charlotte mused.

"You attended the theatre with Mr. Darcy, Lizzy?" Maria asked. "I thought you went with Jane and the Gardiners."

"No, Maria, Mr. Darcy was there with his own party. We simply saw one another in the crowd after the performance, as everyone was leaving."

"Then why does Lady Catherine think you attempted . . . I am not even certain what she was insinuating, to tell the truth." Charlotte paused. "Whatever happened?"

"Nothing, really. Mr. Darcy and I saw one another, and when the crowd became a crush, he was pushed into me. He apologised, I forgave him, and that was that. I cannot imagine why Lady Catherine is so overset." All true. Without context, but true.

Charlotte's gaze was steady and questioning, but Sir William and Maria accepted her explanation easily enough.

"You know how these things are often misconstrued, Miss Elizabeth," Sir William said, lifting his shoulders. "Everyone in Meryton knows what a proper young woman you are, but people in London are different."

"I thank you, Sir William," Elizabeth said, and she meant it.

"I do not think I will like London," Maria said softly. "Had *I* been at the theatre, I would be sure to step wrong without even being aware."

"You will like it, perhaps when you are a little older, Maria," Elizabeth replied. "Do not allow the fear of a simple mistake to rob you of the joy a play or concert might bring."

Maria nodded, but she was clearly dubious. They all sat at the table, their dessert abandoned, and looked at one another.

"Well, that was a rather sad ending to our dinner," Charlotte said at last.

"I am only sorry that we shall not be able to have our visit," Elizabeth said ruefully.

"As am I," Charlotte said. "Papa, Maria? Given that Eliza must leave us in the morning, would you mind very much if I devote myself to her this evening?"

"Of course you want to have your chat," Sir William said, and Maria agreed. Having finished what they could of their food, the two Lucases expressed their dismay that Elizabeth's visit would be cut so short and then bade her a good night.

"Would you like to send an express to your uncle, Eliza, and tell him that we shall send John and Agnes with you?"

It would be inconvenient for Charlotte to have John and Agnes away all day, but there was nothing else to be done. Elizabeth could not take the post alone. Her uncle had intended to send a manservant from his own staff when she and Maria returned, but there was not enough time for him to arrive, and she did not wish to chance another meeting with Lady Catherine were she to remain. Charlotte had been brave, but she would need time to make amends with her husband. "With your permission, I will pen a note telling my family to expect me."

This was soon accomplished, and once John was sent off to hire an express rider, Charlotte offered Elizabeth her arm. They made their way slowly out into the hall, passing the open doorway of the front parlour. Even in the dark, Elizabeth could make out Mr. Collins still standing at the window with one hand pressed to the glass, like a child waving a sad farewell.

Chapter Seven

When Elizabeth had related everything that had happened at the theatre, Charlotte sat back.

"That is quite a tale," she said, shaking her head and offering Elizabeth a little smile. "I thank you for entrusting me with it."

"I do not think I would have, had Lady Catherine not made such a scene in your house. Not because I would not wish to," she added hurriedly when a brief flash of hurt crossed Charlotte's countenance, "but because I have been attempting to forget the entire incident."

"Dear Eliza, there will be no way for this to be kept a secret now."

"I agree. The servants . . ."

"Not only the servants. Lady Catherine has a number of influential friends in town, and I fear that letters are being penned even as we speak."

This had not occurred to Elizabeth. "I dare not suppose these are women who possess more sense and decorum than the mistress of Rosings?"

"I do not know them, of course. Our only evidence is that they maintain correspondence with Lady Catherine."

This was enough. Elizabeth dropped her head into her hands.

"I will of course counter those stories in Hertfordshire as well as I can by writing my mother a more flattering account."

"Perhaps your father will as well."

"I will make certain he does. And I will mention it to Maria."

"Thank you."

"Let us speak of other things," Elizabeth begged her friend, and for a while, they did. They canvassed Elizabeth's concern for Jane but also other, more mundane subjects that only friends of long-standing would find of interest. Charlotte explained that she quite enjoyed running her home, keeping the accounts, tending to parishioners in need. Although she did not say as much, Elizabeth inferred that the other ladies in the congregation already looked to Charlotte as a leader among them. And why not? Charlotte's talents had never been appreciated at Lucas Lodge.

Elizabeth now understood with greater clarity what would drive a woman like her dear friend to wed a man like Mr. Collins. It was a strange thing, to tie oneself to a man to gain some measure of freedom and maddening that this was the only way to go about it. Yet Charlotte had made a place for herself.

Feeling again all the anxiety of what Charlotte's decision to protect her might cost, Elizabeth said, tentatively, "When you said Lady Catherine could not materially affect your husband's livelihood . . ."

Charlotte put her hand over Elizabeth's. "I truly meant it. You need not worry for us, Eliza. Mr. Collins may require a period of mourning . . ."

The women smiled at one another.

"But I cannot repine the improvement this will make to his relationships with his congregants. I am very sure that when the break is known that they will respect him more. And I shall guide him in the best way to go about making it known."

"You are a wonder, Charlotte."

"It is an excellent thing," her friend said, "to be at liberty to put my mind to use in such endeavours. Now, let me help you with your ankle before we say good night. The post leaves not long after breakfast."

Darcy stared into the flinty countenance of a short, thin, hungry-looking man.

"You see 'im, you tell 'im Ratherton would like a word."

No luck. This was the fourth and final place Darcy had known to look. They should never have bothered to leave the house after dinner; he was exhausted from the abrupt journey into and back from Kent earlier in the day. "Thank you," Darcy said formally, and passed the man a coin.

"That is not to be counted against what he owes," Fitzwilliam commented.

The man's laugh was hard and bitter. "This ain't a drop in the ocean of what 'e owes."

It was past midnight when Darcy handed his hat over to his butler and walked into his study. He lit a few candles while Fitzwilliam poured out two glasses of brandy.

"He has gone to ground," Fitzwilliam said with an almost feral smile. "We shall dig him out."

"You enjoy this sort of thing, I think," Darcy said, taking the drink his cousin held out.

"I admit I do. Particularly when our prey is someone I have wished to meet with for some time."

"He must be in deep arrears if he is not even visiting his usual gambling hells."

"Which means either that he has returned to Hertfordshire or he is plucking his next goose."

"Or both."

"We shall have to visit Mrs. Younge."

He knew Fitzwilliam was right. He had men keeping track of her. They would be able to direct him.

"I will inquire." Darcy gazed down into the amber liquid.

"Too bad you did not keep up with your acquaintances in Hertfordshire. You could have written to see whether Wickham was there."

"Too suspicious. They might have alerted him to our interest."

"Perhaps," Fitzwilliam sipped his drink and relaxed into his chair.

Darcy had left Hertfordshire without a backwards glance. For the first time, he wondered whether anyone had been sorry to see him go.

"A pity Miss Elizabeth Bennet is currently in Kent. You said the officers were invited to many of the neighbourhood's events. Surely one of her sisters would know if he had returned."

"Fitzwilliam . . ." The sudden ache that squeezed Darcy's heart at the sound of her name also prompted him to recall their earlier visitor. He reached into his jacket pocket and fingered the card Mr. Gardiner had given him. "Miss Elizabeth may be in Kent, but her uncle is in London."

"After everything he did to appear here unnoticed, you cannot be seen at his door. Not if you want to tamp down speculation."

"I thought you liked him," Darcy said drily. "And her."

Fitzwilliam tossed his head back and contemplated the ceiling. "I do not *know* her," he said, frustrated. "You seem to like her, and that is rare enough. However, you have said you do not wish to make an offer. My loyalty is to you and to what you have said that you want."

"If it were only a question of what I wish . . ."

His cousin grunted. "It *is*. Everything else is merely dealing with the consequences."

"Merely? Georgiana will be out in a year and a half. She will never make the match she can aspire to now if I marry a squire's daughter."

"Yes," the colonel said wryly. "A great match to an earl or viscount, or perhaps even the second son of a duke! To be required to host the aristocracy and be a leading light in the ton! That is precisely what would make Georgiana happiest. I could see at dinner that she wishes for nothing but to be the centre of our attention."

He was right, of course. Georgiana had always been shy in company. Even before Ramsgate, she was not the sort to seek attention. She would rather marry a man who would keep her in the country most of the year, who would allow her to manage his home, raise his children, and attend to her music. In a variety of indirect ways, his sister had told him as much, but Darcy had always considered it her duty as well as his to marry well.

But what did that mean, precisely?

Darcy let his head fall against the back of his chair. His sister's character was a quiet one. That would not change. "Georgiana would like Miss Elizabeth."

Perhaps it was because Darcy had not slept well after the incident at the theatre and was now debating whether he had enough strength left to make the stairs to his chamber, but he found himself considering the possibility of introducing them.

"Then why hesitate?" Fitzwilliam asked, his voice rough and his eyes closing. "We might end all this exhausting subterfuge at once if you simply called openly once she returns from Kent."

"You are trying to raise your father's ire and make me the target."

"Father will be disappointed. Mother will be curious. Milton will be amused and forever remind you of your diminished status. Your friends will either laugh at you or shake their heads, for they shall think you have thrown yourself away, and you may not be invited to join certain investments for fear that your judgement is impaired." His cousin's voice began to fade. "The question is, do you care?"

Darcy allowed his own eyes to drift shut. The investments would be a nuisance, but he would survive. Georgiana might even be pleased. As for the rest? "I do," he said honestly. "But perhaps not enough."

Elizabeth's heart raced with panic. "What do you mean, the post has gone?" she asked dumbly.

The woman behind the counter shrugged. "It comes through first thing, ma'am, same time every day."

Elizabeth turned to Charlotte. "You said the post came later."

"Well," Charlotte said, pressing her lips together, "I am still new here."

Charlotte only pressed her lips together when she was attempting to hide something. What was she about? "Charlotte . . ."

"Yes?" her friend asked innocently.

"What have you done?"

"Whatever do you mean?"

Elizabeth shook her head. "Please do not pretend ignorance, it does not become you. You have a plan."

"For now, perhaps we should just walk home."

"I cannot return to the parsonage, Charlotte, not after last night. Your husband might well suffer an apoplexy if I did."

Her friend smiled a little. "He will remain in his study until I can assure him that you have gone. But let us see if we can devise something better."

Elizabeth glared at Charlotte. "This is hardly helpful."

"Agnes," Charlotte called to the maid who had accompanied them, "come along."

"What about my trunks?"

"John will see to them." Charlotte nodded at the manservant, who touched his hat and hefted one of Elizabeth's two trunks over his shoulder as though it weighed nothing.

When they stepped outside, Elizabeth squinted in the bright light of the sun and shivered a bit, for the air was still cold. Spring was coming, and it saddened her that she would not be welcoming it here. From what little she had seen of it, she could say that Kent was a beautiful place.

"Hello, Mr. Anders!" Charlotte called.

Elizabeth froze, and it had nothing to do with the weather.

Mr. Darcy's sleek black carriage had been nowhere in sight when they entered to purchase her ticket for the post, but now it sat just a few feet away. Two footmen waited alongside with the spry young coachman atop it. No one was inside.

Mr. Anders lifted his hat and climbed down when he spied them.

"Good day, Mrs. Collins. I received your note this morning." He touched the brim of his hat. "Miss Bennet."

Elizabeth smiled. "Good day, Mr. Anders. I believed you had returned to London yesterday."

"No, miss. Mr. Darcy would never abuse his horses in such a way. They have had a brushing, a meal, and a rest overnight up at Rosings. I am only sorry that these"—he pressed his lips together, no doubt to prevent using some colourful language—"these men, brought unsupported rumours to Rosings." He glared at Mr. Darcy's footmen who did, indeed, appear abashed.

"No harm was meant, ma'am," one said, touching his hat. "It was just seeing the master so attentive, is all."

Mr. Anders cut the man off with a sharp word, and he fell silent. John began to strap her trunk to the back of the coach, and both footmen turned to help.

"Charlotte," she hissed, though she already understood, "what is John doing?"

"He is securing your trunks. I was afraid we might miss the post, and as you see, Mr. Anders is for London this very moment. It will work out quite nicely."

"Miss Bennet," Mr. Anders said, glancing between the two of them. "Forgive me, but I am certain Mr. Darcy would insist upon my conveying you safely home."

She could not remain here. It would certainly cause additional grief for Charlotte were Elizabeth to beg a return to the parsonage, a poor thanks for the courage her friend had displayed on her behalf. Truly, she did not wish to return.

She had no choice. She nodded to accept the offer, and Mr. Anders tipped his hat and walked away to speak with John.

She pulled Charlotte around the corner of the building to have a private word with her. "How long did it take for you to devise this plan?" she asked grimly.

"Not long," her friend confessed. "Lady Catherine mentioned her information came from servants, and hers never leave Rosings." She patted Elizabeth's hand. "I was very unhappy thinking of you travelling post without even Maria to accompany you inside the box."

"That is not the reason, Charlotte, and you know it."

"Not the *only* reason," Charlotte conceded. "My concern for your welfare on the journey back to Gracechurch Street soon grew into a concern for your welfare in more general terms. Eliza," she said solemnly, "when Lady Catherine has done her worst, there will be no way for you to repair your family's good name in London. You must consider the obvious alternative to discretion."

"Which is?"

"Eliza, you are not slow-witted. That man watched you a great deal during his time in Hertfordshire. I recall pointing that out to you."

"It will not matter. Even if Mr. Darcy were so inclined, his family"—she waved vaguely in the direction of Rosings—"would interfere."

"Elizabeth." Charlotte never used her full name. She must be very serious indeed.

"Yes?"

"You have done Mr. Darcy a great service. He will move to stop Lady Catherine by offering you his hand."

"You are wrong, Charlotte. Even if you were not, would either of us be happy in such a match?"

"If I can find contentment," Charlotte told her firmly, "so can you."

"Charlotte . . ." Elizabeth did not want to be content. She wanted to be *happy*. Her parents' marriage was a constant reminder of the dangers of an unequal alliance.

"Your mind," Charlotte said, interrupting, "is too quick, too clever for the men in your circle in Hertfordshire. And forgive me, but your father will never bestir himself to take you to London for a proper season, though he could certainly afford a modest one for you and for Jane."

Elizabeth did not wish to admit that Charlotte was right about Papa, but she was an honest woman, so she only offered a small nod.

"Against all odds, Mr. Darcy came to Hertfordshire. He is a clever man, a good match for you—and you have captured his interest."

"I do not believe that, Charlotte."

Charlotte was undeterred. "You have both made a valiant attempt to keep this incident of yours private, but your efforts have utterly failed. He is not a bad man, though he may be a proud one. He will offer."

Elizabeth shook her head, on the verge of tears but not allowing them to fall.

"Think, Eliza," Charlotte said, giving her a little shake before letting her hands drop. "You will soon be seen returning from Kent in Mr. Darcy's carriage and being safely delivered to your uncle Gardiner's door, which announces to those who would malign you that Mr. Darcy does not agree with his aunt's treatment of you."

"But he will not know until after the deed is done."

"He will not be angry, for it is his own servants who have gossiped and his own aunt who has sent you away." Charlotte took a deep breath. "If Mr. Darcy did not think well of you, he might easily have sent help back for you yesterday rather than give up his own carriage. And were he intending to offer you a proposition of a different sort . . ."

"*Charlotte!*" Elizabeth lifted her hands to her burning cheeks.

"Forgive me, dear. I have seen a great deal in the short time I have been a pastor's wife, and I do not believe that gentlewomen should be kept in ignorance." She allowed Elizabeth to regain her composure before continuing. "If Mr. Darcy sought *that* sort of arrangement, he would never have allowed you to ride to the parsonage, a stone's throw from Rosings, in a carriage emblazoned with his family crest."

"You *do* wish to force Mr. Darcy to make an offer for me."

"I hope to see to your happiness, dear. Yours and his."

"He *may* pay my father a settlement. He will not offer."

Their time was growing short. If Elizabeth was going to take Mr. Darcy's carriage, they would have to leave before Lady Catherine was informed, and word was certainly already winging its way up to the great house.

"This is the life I sought," Charlotte said quietly, gesturing around them, "and I am happy. But you have always been meant for something more, Eliza. You cannot deny that you yearn for it."

Elizabeth could not.

"I believe with all my heart that you will make Mr. Darcy a charming, intelligent, loving wife, and I wish to see you as free to use your gifts as I am now. More so, for your husband's influence will be greater." She pressed Elizabeth's hands. "It is precisely the sort of life that will suit you best, Eliza, and I daresay you will never have such an opportunity again."

She did not inform Charlotte that Mr. Collins had employed a very similar warning.

There was nothing for it at any rate. The post was gone, and Mr. Darcy's carriage was her only escape.

Only a few days before, she would have been convinced of Mr. Darcy's implacable resentment. But no more. The man had graciously, if somewhat officiously, offered to stand with her at the theatre. He had been determined to see her safely out of the theatre when they had believed there was a fire. The very next day he had offered her party the use of his carriage to take them to Hunsford, though their predicament was neither his fault nor his responsibility. Even his sharp words about Mr. Wickham had taken on new meaning. Mr. Darcy had not been haughty there; he had, in his own way, been warning her.

Elizabeth closed her eyes and shuddered at the memory of his strong hand gently turning her face to one side. Of the way those strong, capable hands had nearly encircled her waist . . .

She opened her eyes to see her friend smiling knowingly at her, and Elizabeth remembered spending half an hour in the library at Netherfield while Mr. Darcy ignored her entirely.

"He will not offer for me, Charlotte," Elizabeth repeated doggedly. "This I can say for certain."

Chapter Eight

"Carriage or horses?" Fitzwilliam inquired after Georgiana went upstairs to prepare for her music master's weekly visit and the footmen were temporarily out of the room.

"Neither is a good option," Darcy said. He sighed. "I do not expect the carriage to return for some hours yet, and it is the only one I keep in town."

"It has your crest on it, in any case."

"We might take a hackney. It could excite notice, but then being atop our horses would make us far easier to identify."

"Hackney it is, then."

Darcy never travelled in a hackney if it could be avoided. To do so required suffering excruciatingly close quarters in an inferior coach. And then there was the problem of trusting one's safety to a driver about whom he was entirely ignorant. But there was nothing for it. Before they expended more resources to continue their search here, they must discover whether Wickham had returned to Meryton.

It was better, at least, than a coal cart.

By noon they were on their way, but the London roads, as always, were difficult to traverse. Their driver made his way through the hordes of carts, coaches, and wagons with a steady hand, but their progress was unbearably slow.

Over an hour later, they finally came to a stop before Gracechurch Street, number fifty. As Darcy paid the driver, Fitzwilliam was already knocking on the front door.

The building was rather handsome, with a black door, red shutters, and a clean, red brick façade. It was a comfortable home between the lighter stone buildings stained dark by the coal smoke that lingered in the London air all winter. Empty wrought iron window boxes promised colour in the spring.

A maid allowed them inside, and Darcy was grateful to see that the hackney driver had already deserted them in search of his next fare. No doubt Mr. Gardiner's staff could locate a new one for the return trip.

He glanced about the entry, which was rather grander than he had expected for a home in this part of town. The floor was a richly veined marble, the wainscoting a snowy white, the walls above boasting a very fine blue damask paper with a raised pattern in silver.

"That is very nearly the same paper Mother has in her private sitting room," Fitzwilliam said, turning to study it. "She would be appalled to know that it adorns the walls here." He smiled. "I think I shall have to tell her."

Darcy stifled a laugh. His aunt was a good woman, but like anyone else, she had her little vanities. In her case, it would not be so much that her paper was being used in the home of a tradesman but rather that it was in the home of anyone else at all. She strove for originality.

He took a deep breath and attempted to focus on the matter at hand and not the fact that as recently as yesterday morning, Miss Elizabeth had been walking through this very hall on her way to Kent.

A man with dark brown skin and a stately air approached them. "The master is from home, gentlemen, but Mrs. Gardiner will meet you in the drawing room if you wish."

"We would appreciate the opportunity to meet her," Fitzwilliam said warmly.

Darcy just nodded.

Fitzwilliam tapped Darcy's arm as the man led them down an elegantly decorated hall. He appeared to be in his early forties, his shoulders broad and his bearing upright.

"I should not like to meet *him* at Gentleman Jack's," Fitzwilliam whispered.

They were shown into a splendid formal drawing room. Its dimensions were generous, nearly equalling the size of Darcy's own public drawing room here in town.

In the centre of the room was a thick wool rug, on each side of which were silk settees, and upon the far one, facing the door were two women who rose to greet their visitors. The elder was only a few years older than himself, Darcy thought. She was quite pretty and certainly genteel, well dressed for daytime callers, her auburn hair curled about her head in a simple but becoming style.

Next to her was a woman he knew, her blonde hair put up in a slightly more elaborate style. A single long curl trailed down the elegant line of her neck, and a few shorter curls framed her perfectly symmetrical face.

Darcy swallowed, and his palms felt damp. He had entirely forgotten Miss Bennet was in residence. How addle-pated he had become in the past few days!

Fitzwilliam let out a startled little breath but quickly recovered himself.

"Welcome, Mr. Darcy," the first woman said. "I am Mrs. Gardiner, and this is my niece, Miss Bennet. If you would care to wait with us, I have sent for my husband. He has been speaking with his man about the weavers."

"Silks," Darcy said. He sounded touched. There was silk in the wall coverings. His aunt's study was adorned by paper sold by Mr. Gardiner.

Fitzwilliam chuckled. "Colonel Fitzwilliam, madam. Miss Bennet. I see you already know my eloquent cousin."

Miss Bennet offered Fitzwilliam a small smile, but Darcy could see the small lines of strain near her eyes, and he wondered at them.

"Your husband offered us a small list of his businesses," Fitzwilliam said.

Mrs. Gardiner smiled. "Yes, he finds it humorous, I daresay. Will you not be seated?"

"Thank you," Fitzwilliam said. He gave Darcy a hard stare until he echoed his cousin and took a seat on the settee facing the ladies.

He needed to take hold of himself. "It is a pleasure to see you again, Miss Bennet. I hope your family is well."

"You have lately seen Elizabeth, sir," Miss Bennet said kindly. "And the rest of my family is well, I thank you."

She very pointedly did not ask about the Bingleys or the Hursts. Miss Bingley had severed the acquaintance, then, as she had threatened to do.

"Excellent." Darcy subsided back into silence. His mind was racing. His own complicity in separating Bingley from Miss Bennet stretched only to offering an opinion when asked and not mentioning her presence in town. He had only acted in Bingley's best interests.

As Fitzwilliam kept the conversation lively and pleasant, Darcy was reminded that Miss Elizabeth had the same sort of ease in company as his cousin. Perhaps that was why he was so drawn to her. She had none of the reticence of her sister, just as Fitzwilliam had none of Darcy's . . .

His heart dropped. No, Mrs. Bennet *must* have forced the issue. Miss Bennet did not appear heartbroken. She was pleasant and serene, as she had always been.

But those lines near her eyes were not fading. This call was a struggle for her.

"My cousin is not usually so dull in company," Fitzwilliam said, bringing Darcy back to the present.

"My apologies, Mrs. Gardiner, Miss Bennet. I am afraid that my cousin is happy to speak for both of us, and I allowed my mind to wander."

Miss Bennet laughed softly. "My sister Elizabeth carries the weight of many conversations for me. She is rather quick on her feet. I often require more time to compose a reply."

Fitzwilliam was quick to compliment her. "Ah, but I suspect you are often searching for something kind to say while my cousin's mind is attempting to solve every possible problem of the world and simply misses what he has been asked."

"Thank you," Miss Bennet said quietly.

"Are you a deep thinker, then, Mr. Darcy?" Mrs. Gardiner asked, something very serious lurking just beneath her teasing remark.

How like Miss Elizabeth her aunt was.

Or rather, how much Miss Elizabeth was like . . .

"I suspect Miss Elizabeth and Miss Bennet spent a good deal of time here as girls?"

This startled everyone. Even Fitzwilliam threw an incredulous look at him. Darcy tried not to blush and added, "Forgive my presumption. Miss Elizabeth has mentioned how dear you and your husband are to her."

This was true, after a fashion. He had overheard her through an open door at Netherfield. Miss Bennet had said something about Miss Bingley and Mrs. Hurst asking her questions about their family over dinner the first night she was there, before she had been taken ill. Miss Elizabeth had burst forth with a paean for her relatives in trade. He had not thought much of it then, as caught up as he had been in denying his nascent feelings for her, but now he could understand why she had been so stout in their defence.

"Dear Lizzy," Miss Bennet said affectionately. "She is a great protector of family."

Fitzwilliam nodded. "She seems to have that propensity towards others of her acquaintance as well."

He was prodding Miss Bennet to see what she knew, of course. Darcy could have told him that Miss Elizabeth had no secrets from her elder sister. They were closer than any siblings he had ever met. Although he adored Georgiana, the great difference both in age and sex meant that they were not close confidants.

"Oh," Miss Bennet said, and blushed prettily. "Yes." She offered Darcy an apologetic glance. "Lizzy did tell me about what happened at the theatre, if it is that to which Colonel Fitzwilliam refers."

Darcy had never spoken to Miss Bennet at any length, but he could not be surprised that a sister Miss Elizabeth valued so highly would also be intelligent.

"I would never speak of it, of course," she assured them, "even if it were not of great import to the well-being of my own family to remain discreet."

"I thank you, Miss Bennet," Fitzwilliam said. He glanced at Darcy and then turned his attention back to the women. "I know not how this will all end, but I would, if possible, preserve the luxury of choice for both your sister and my cousin."

"I believe," Mrs. Gardiner said wryly, "that will not be difficult in Elizabeth's case. She is not a woman to be forced into anything she does not wish."

Miss Bennet laughed softly. "That, my dear aunt, is an understatement of nearly biblical proportions."

"Really?" Fitzwilliam asked, curiosity and smugness mingled together as he sat back. "Do tell."

"Well," Miss Bennet began thoughtfully, "Lizzy's stubbornness is a very essential part of her character. For example, she is not a great admirer of heights."

"Should we be speaking of Elizabeth when she is not here to speak for herself?" Mrs. Gardiner said, gently chiding her niece.

"Perhaps not," Miss Bennet said, moving the gaze of her clear blue eyes to Darcy's and holding it there. "But I wish Mr. Darcy to be aware that her bravery the other night was even greater than he suspects."

"I see," Mrs. Gardiner said. "I will not stop you, then."

"Do you mean she is afraid, Miss Bennet?" Fitzwilliam inquired, his interest clearly piqued.

"When she was a girl, she was quite paralyzed by her fear, Colonel."

"But Miss Elizabeth would not allow such a thing to rule her," Darcy mumbled.

"No, sir," Miss Bennet said, lifting her chin. "She allows nothing to intimidate her." Darcy nodded. *Or anyone.*

"She set out to climb the highest trees, to climb Oakham Mount near our home. She even sat upon the roof of Longbourn more than once to identify the constellations."

"You are saying," Darcy replied, wishing Miss Bennet to understand that her point had been made, "that she would have been afraid of the stairs at the theatre." They *were* a treacherous set of steps.

"She has not yet entirely overcome her fear. Even so, she did not allow that to keep her from coming to your aid, sir. *That* is my sister."

Miss Elizabeth was not the only protector in the Bennet family. Given that their parents were by turns indolent and inappropriate, it was no wonder.

"I thank you, Miss Bennet. I am very grateful to your sister, but I was not at liberty to speak with her then as I would have wished."

"I understand, sir. I should be pleased to convey your gratitude in my next letter if you wish."

"Thank you again. I would appreciate that."

Miss Bennet smiled, satisfied. "Then I shall."

Voices came from the hall, and Mr. Gardiner soon showed himself in the drawing room. His expression was less pleasant than their welcome had been.

"Gentlemen, would you care to join me in my study?"

Chapter Nine

"We would, sir," Darcy replied, standing. "Miss Bennet, I thank you for enlightening me. Mrs. Gardiner, your servant."

The women rose and bid him a warm farewell. Fitzwilliam said all that was polite, and then they followed Mr. Gardiner down another splendid hall where smaller landscape portraits lined one wall and several excellent marble busts, including Diana and Apollo facing one another, were set into the wall at regular intervals. The ceilings were high and the hall a little wide, giving the impression of great space, something Darcy did not always experience, being as tall as he was. The study was on another wing of the house, and as they walked, they passed through where the wall ought to have been. Mr. Gardiner had both number 50 and number 52, something not noticeable from the street.

Fitzwilliam was taking everything in though he was silent. Mr. Gardiner must have many expenses, living in London as he did without the benefit of a home garden for food or trees for wood to heat his home. To afford such a residence despite this meant his income must be quite comfortable indeed. It belied any notion that Miss Bingley might hold dear about the family's financial circumstances.

"Now," Mr. Gardiner said, sweeping one hand at the chairs sitting before his desk and taking his own seat behind it, "I admit I am perplexed. After the lengths I went to yesterday to deliver my niece's message, I did not expect you two to arrive at my doorstep today. In the bright light of midday, no less."

"We arrived in a hackney, sir," Darcy said, wishing him to know that they had not taken his own sacrifice of dignity for granted. "We do not believe anyone has recognised us."

His cousin picked up where Darcy had left off. "Unfortunately, we could not trust a servant to deliver our message any more than you could trust one to deliver yours."

"And that message is?"

"Well, it is a question, really," Fitzwilliam amended.

"Mm." Mr. Gardiner eyed them suspiciously.

"We were unable to find Wickham on our first foray. Before we continue to search for him here, we would like to know whether he has, in fact, returned to Meryton."

"And you would like me to write to my brother to ask?"

That was not what Darcy would have asked, and he grimaced at the misunderstanding. There was every probability that Mr. Bennet would have no idea.

"I see you comprehend the problem, Mr. Darcy," Mr. Gardiner said flatly. "My brother does not participate in his community as often as he should."

"I mean no offense, sir."

He waved his hand, dismissing the apology. "You have given none. The best course would be to ask Jane. She receives regular letters from her mother, who would be more likely to list the name of every officer who has visited the house."

"I confess, that is precisely what I had hoped," Darcy told him.

"I shall put it to her, then." He rose. "You may remain here," he told them in a tone that invited no dissension. He paused for a moment to stare at Darcy with a bit of cool displeasure. "My sister writes of who has *not* been to call as well. Endlessly."

Darcy met the man's gaze unflinchingly, but he felt the hit to his own conscience.

When the door shut behind Mr. Gardiner, Fitzwilliam stood. "I can see how he runs so many businesses."

Darcy agreed. He already respected Miss Elizabeth's uncle despite the dawning realisation that the man did not much admire him. It was not a comfortable feeling.

Fitzwilliam turned to examine a still life that hung on the wall. "I say, these paintings are very good." He paused. "This is a Mary Moser! I daresay those in the entry hall are just as impressive. By the by," he continued without turning around, "were I Bingley, I would plant you a facer for separating me from that goddess in the drawing room."

"Yes, well. I did not doubt Bingley's affection so much as hers."

"One day, Darcy" Fitzwilliam said warningly, "you will have to allow him to manage his life without your interference."

That smarted. "I do not interfere. I was asked for my opinion, and I gave it."

"Who asked? Bingley or his sister?"

That hit rather squarely. Darcy sighed. "Bingley, but his sister instigated the conversation. I will say that Miss Bennet appeared differently today than she has before."

"I would imagine so. She was tense. Anxious. Unhappy. Yet never once did she mention Bingley or his sister, no doubt because to do so might cause *you* discomfort. Yet when she had the opportunity, she made certain you understood just how wonderful her sister is. She is a proper lady and not without spirit."

"I agree."

"Then you owe Bingley the knowledge that she is in town."

He knew it. "It will have to be soon. Bingley is readying to travel north to a house party." He paused. "I cannot speak of this to Miss Bennet or her family. I would not wish to excite any expectations. Bingley may decide not to act upon my information."

"If he does, I shall think him not merely a young fool, but a great one."

"As you consider me?" Darcy considered himself a fool in all things Miss Elizabeth Bennet, that much was certain.

"You are not a fool, Darcy," Fitzwilliam said, clasping his hands behind his back and turning, at last, to face him. "You are conceited."

"I beg your pardon?"

"That exquisite pile of yours blinds you to the fact that your family is not the highest in England."

"I thank you, but Milton reminds me of that nearly every time we meet. Believe me, I am aware."

"My brother the viscount is not even the highest rank in your extended family," Fitzwilliam reminded him. "The Darcys are wealthy and powerful, but they are not peers."

"Have you a point to make, Fitzwilliam?" Darcy was both annoyed and frustrated.

Fitzwilliam cocked his head to one side and ignored the question. "You are also not the smartest man in the country, though you often pretend such."

"I readily concede that I am not the cleverest man in England." Easy enough to do, especially when he had spent months struggling over what should have been a simple decision.

"I will add that when it comes to women . . ."

Here it was at last, and Darcy finished the sentence. "I am, in fact, the stupidest?"

Fitzwilliam chuckled. "Middle of the pack. Your position as Georgie's guardian has saved you from a more dismal showing."

Darcy was not at all sure of that.

The door opened, and Darcy stood. Mr. Gardiner strode back into the room and assessed them keenly. "Jane says that in her last letter, her mother related her disappointment that Mr. Wickham and Captain Denny were being sent to London for a fortnight on militia business. The letter was received only two days ago. I have asked her to write in the morning to discreetly confirm this, but in the meantime, I believe we may presume that the man is still here."

"Why, this is excellent!" Fitzwilliam cried. "I had believed we should have to wait for letters back and forth."

"My sister is a very thorough correspondent," Mr. Gardiner said drolly. He exchanged a knowing glance with Darcy.

"You must understand, sirs," he said, addressing them both, though Darcy was aware that the information was primarily for his sake, "that although my sister may at times behave irrationally, that behaviour has steadily worsened over the years. Longbourn's heir is a distant relation, you see, and she is anxious for her future and that of her daughters."

"Does she know how well you get on, Mr. Gardiner?" Fitzwilliam asked directly.

The man smiled. "I do not believe she fully understands, but we do try to assuage her concerns. Neither she nor any unmarried daughters will ever be reduced to genteel poverty. But neither will she live as she does now, and having to cede her position as mistress of Longbourn to another woman would be difficult for her."

Fitzwilliam was generous. "It would be difficult for any woman."

Darcy understood the expression upon Mr. Gardiner's countenance, but he was not allowed time to commiserate, for the man was ready to be shot of them.

"Does that conclude our business, gentlemen?"

"Not entirely," Darcy said, intending to inform Mr. Gardiner about their meeting with Miss Elizabeth the day before. "We ought to have said something last night, in fact."

"About?" There was a loud knock at the door. Mr. Gardiner frowned. "Come in," he called.

The same manservant who had led them to the drawing room stepped inside now and spoke quietly with Mr. Gardiner.

"Are you certain?" Miss Elizabeth's uncle exclaimed.

"Mrs. Gardiner confirms it, sir."

A deep, bone-rattling sigh escaped from his employer. "Thank you, Vaz." He dismissed the butler and turned to glare at Darcy. "It appears," he said, "that your carriage has arrived."

"Not only that, Miss Elizabeth," Agnes said effusively, "but Mr. Darcy made sure all the accounts were satisfied, which was a great relief to the merchants, and he increased pay for most of the servants, depending upon their position and their time with the family, of course."

Some hours ago, Elizabeth had asked Agnes what she knew of Mr. Darcy. While Agnes was at first reluctant to speak, Elizabeth had provided her with a ready ear, which was apparently all that was required. Now Agnes could not seem to stop. Even her dialect moved back and forth between the proper English she would be expected to use at the parsonage and the more familiar accents she likely used when among her family.

"Lady Catherine does not believe in raising pay, she says it makes servants grasping, you know. But Mr. Darcy told her quite direct that she should have no servants at all if she insisted on such paltry wages, and that she ought not expect *him* to do the cooking."

Elizabeth chuckled. "Did he truly say that?"

"Oh, yes, Miss Elizabeth. My brother, he's a footman, you see, on account of him being quite tall—he was in the room at the time and had a good laugh about it later, he did. He says Mr. Darcy is normally very kind to his aunt, but he were just that exasperated with her."

Agnes glanced out the window.

With Agnes finally falling silent and nothing else to divert her attention, Elizabeth felt again the nagging pains from the injuries of her past few days. She greatly anticipated having a hot bath this evening to soothe her aching back. Her aunt would see to a cool cloth for the bruise near her jaw that was currently concealed behind a few carefully arranged curls and some ice for the ankle that still throbbed a bit every time the carriage hit a rut in the road. Even Mr. Anders, it would seem, could not completely avoid them, and now they were rattling over the cobblestones, which were not a great deal better.

Despite her pains, she could not stop thinking of all Agnes had told her. Evidently the servants at Rosings thought very highly of Mr. Darcy, and why would they not? According to Agnes, he was the one ensuring that they were treated well, including being properly compensated for their work. To have such a reputation among the servants was quite rare.

"Is Mr. Darcy often at Rosings, Agnes?" she asked.

"No, ma'am, just near Easter. It's the best time of the year, my brother says, when Mr. Darcy and Colonel Fitzwilliam come to Rosings."

"The colonel comes every year as well?"

"He does, ma'am. Often makes a tour of the estate, speaks to the tenants while Mr. Darcy is so busy with the books and all. They ride out together sometimes, too."

It amused Elizabeth to hear that Mr. Darcy's schedule was so closely observed. Even a footman's sister who did not work in his aunt's home still knew its general outline. A moment later, she felt a twinge of conscience as she cast her thoughts back to the assembly last autumn, where rumours of Mr. Darcy's worth had circulated the room before he had even had a moment to introduce himself to his host. It might be amusing to her, but how difficult it must be for him, reticent as he was. No wonder he had been ill at ease. It did not excuse his rudeness, of course, but perhaps it did explain it a bit.

Agnes chattered on merrily. Although Mr. Darcy was expected every year around Easter for a family visit, in truth, it seemed that he and the colonel arrived mostly to correct everything that Lady Catherine had spent the rest of the year putting wrong.

"It is Lady Catherine's estate, of course, so Mr. Darcy does not always have his way." Agnes tipped her head up in thought. "But when it has to do with how she treats the staff, ma'am, he insists upon it. And Lady Catherine, she goes along with him though she will not listen to anyone else. I think it's on account of how she wants him to marry Miss de Bourgh."

"I had heard that they were engaged," Elizabeth ventured to say.

"None of us believe it, for my brother says Mr. Darcy hardly sees Miss de Bourgh when he comes," Agnes declared with a cheerful grin. "But Lady Catherine does seem to *like* the idea."

"And Miss de Bourgh?"

"It's the colonel who sits with her more than Mr. Darcy. He's able to get her to laugh a bit, poor thing. Mr. Darcy, for all he is a good man, is very serious. My brother hardly sees Miss de Bourgh in the public rooms when her cousins are away. Says she seems rather sickly and ought not marry anyone."

The footman's thoughts were the same as Charlotte's, then.

"In my opinion, and you mustn't tell anyone, miss . . ." Agnes awaited her promise, which was freely given, "Miss de Bourgh is not so sick as she looks, for she is quite fearless in her phaeton when she don't think anyone is watching."

"You have seen her?"

"Of course. The paths by the parsonage are far enough from Rosings that she would not be seen there. Her companion would never tell, and we wouldn't either. Not even my brother knows." Agnes frowned. "Mr. Darcy is the one who told Lady Catherine that his cousin ought to ride out whenever she chose. Good for her health, he said, and Lady Catherine allowed it! Poor thing," she said again, "not even able to go outside without permission. No wonder she takes that little bit of freedom for a run now and again." She shook her head resolutely. "I know Miss de Bourgh has a great deal of money, but for all that, I do not believe I would change places with her."

Elizabeth's shame increased. Though she had never met Miss de Bourgh, she had already judged her based upon information she had received from Mr. Wickham, who she now knew to be a dishonourable man. She had done that while Agnes had found it in her heart to feel sympathy instead. Elizabeth made a vow to herself that she would endeavour to be a better person.

As she listened to all the wonderful things Mr. Darcy had done to assist the staff at Rosings, that sense of shame grew apace. She had not repeated Mr. Wickham's accusations to anyone in Hertfordshire beyond Jane and Charlotte. However, despite his declaration that he could not demean the son for fear of dishonouring the father, Mr. Wickham had spread his lies about freely once the Netherfield party had left for London. She could see it so clearly now, how Mr. Wickham had taken advantage. Jane's disappointment had been widely discussed, and he had used the general indignation on her behalf to smear Mr. Darcy's name and earn compassion for himself that he did not deserve.

Even Miss Bingley had known better, warning her that Mr. Wickham was not a man to be trusted. That rankled worst of all.

Agnes spoke about the tenants next, but even there it appeared that the colonel's job was mostly to take what he had learned to Darcy, who was better versed in how to assist them than his military cousin.

It felt an age before Mr. Anders deftly pulled the carriage to a stop in front of her uncle's door, but how much she had learned! Elizabeth was very grateful to be back once more at Gracechurch Street. She was cold and weary to the bone, and it was not only due to her extended travels.

She needed her gentle sister to tell her she was not so very bad, and if anyone could help her sort through her conflicted feelings for a certain gentleman from Derbyshire, it was her aunt Gardiner.

One of Mr. Darcy's footmen helped her from the carriage and offered her an arm when he saw she was having a little trouble walking. Agnes took the steps after her, suddenly quiet and demure once again.

They entered the house just as her aunt and Jane were coming out to meet them. "Elizabeth!" cried her aunt. "What in the world?"

Jane embraced her, causing Elizabeth to teeter to the side and put too much weight on her ankle. She gasped.

"What have you done to yourself?" Jane inquired, pulling away but keeping hold of Elizabeth's right arm.

"And why," her aunt asked, reaching to take the other, "are you arriving here in Mr. Darcy's carriage?"

"It is a long story, Aunt," she said.

"One I should like to hear," her uncle said from a few feet down the hall.

Elizabeth looked up, intending to reply. But her uncle was not alone.

He was instead flanked by two other gentlemen of her acquaintance, one sandy-haired and squarely built, the other darker, taller, broad at the shoulders but slim at the waist. This latter was the very man she had once told her aunt would never be caught visiting such a low place as Gracechurch Street. Yet here he was.

"Mr. Darcy," she said. "Whatever are you doing here?" Her tone was *almost* accusatory, but she was not angry with him, not anymore, only tired and wishing for a hot bath. Unfortunately, it seemed that neither rest nor a soak were in her immediate future.

"I might ask the same of you, Elizabeth," her uncle said.

Chapter Ten

"This time, Uncle, it was not my fault," Elizabeth insisted.

"You bear no blame for our meeting at the theatre either," Mr. Darcy said. Why had she never noticed how smooth and deep his voice was? It struck her then—her uncle must have delivered her message, for how else would Mr. Darcy know where to find them?

"Perhaps we might all repair to a more private room?" Mrs. Gardiner suggested.

"Indeed," Mr. Darcy's cousin said quickly. "Ladies?"

Mr. Darcy stepped outside to speak with his coachman.

"Did not you receive my note, Aunt?" Elizabeth asked quietly, as they made their way behind the men to the drawing room. "John was supposed to have sent it last night."

Agnes, who had descended from the carriage behind Elizabeth, nodded in support.

"No," Mrs. Gardiner whispered. "We had no such missive."

"Pardon me, miss," Agnes said quietly, "but if John weren't able to find a rider so late, he'd have left it to be brought this morning."

Too late to do any good now, of course. So quickly had she been expelled from the parsonage that they had travelled in advance of the express.

Elizabeth glanced out of the window. Mr. Anders was already speaking with Mr. Darcy while the footmen removed her trunks. No one who was at all acquainted with the Darcy family could fail to notice.

"Agnes wishes to visit her family while we are here, Aunt Gardiner," Elizabeth said. "I believe they live rather close?"

"Aye, not far, miss," Agnes said.

"Vaz, would you see that Agnes has something to eat and a way to reach her family when she is ready?" Aunt Gardiner said. "Unless it is very close and you can send someone to escort her, I do not wish to send her on foot."

"Of course, ma'am," Vaz said, offering them all a little bow and departing with Agnes.

Inside the drawing room, Jane and her aunt made her sit down and put her foot up on a pillow, which was everything embarrassing. Mr. Darcy returned just as Jane covered her with a blanket from her waist down for propriety's sake and Mrs. Gardiner sent for some ice and cloths. They all then sat down.

"I am sorry to see that your ankle is no better today," Mr. Darcy said.

"It was improving, but . . ." Elizabeth closed her eyes. But his aunt had sent her off and the carriage ride had been jarring.

This was everything mortifying.

Uncle Gardiner made certain that the door was closed, then ran a hand down his face. "I believe," he said, both his voice and his mien showing considerable strain, "we ought to begin again. We know what happened at the theatre. I should like to hear, in detail, what occurred after Lizzy and the Lucases departed for Kent yesterday morning."

Elizabeth told her part of the story, calming both her sister and her aunt when she informed them how the axle had broken. Jane was quite upset by the danger her sister had so narrowly avoided, and she was unwilling to release Elizabeth's hand for some time.

Mr. Darcy explained that they had come upon her party after the accident and had felt it only right to offer the use of his carriage to Miss Elizabeth's party so that they might complete their journey.

"Knowing that not only was Miss Elizabeth to be in Kent for some weeks but that she would be residing just across the lane from Rosings, my cousin and I naturally turned back to London."

"Naturally," her uncle said.

"My coachman was then obliged to rest the horses overnight, so took them on to Rosings with a message for my aunt telling her not to expect us after all."

There was a brief silence while they all looked at one another.

"Now I should like to know why Miss Elizabeth was in my cousin's carriage today?"

"Fitzwilliam," Darcy said, not appreciating his cousin's tone.

"You are fortunate, Colonel," Miss Elizabeth replied, "for I cannot take offense when I have spent the past four hours hearing great praise of you and Mr. Darcy." She turned her gaze to Mr. Darcy. "Agnes is quite your supporter, sir."

"Agnes?"

Elizabeth smiled. The colonel was confused. "Mrs. Collins's maid."

"Agnes Halloway?" Mr. Darcy asked, his forehead creased in thought.

"The very one."

"Caleb Halloway's sister," he informed the colonel.

Elizabeth laughed, a brief, wild sort of laugh at this evidence supporting Agnes's devotion. Mr. Darcy not only knew the names of the servants at his aunt's home, but he also recalled the name of his aunt's footman's sister. Elizabeth knew the staff and their families at Longbourn, of course, but Rosings was not even his estate.

Everyone looked at her. She supposed the laugh was a little out of tune with the conversation.

"Are you well, Elizabeth?" Her aunt was peering at her with some concern.

Elizabeth pursed her lips and nodded. "A little browbeaten, but intact."

The colonel chuckled, but Mr. Darcy's stare was all flame and heat. Was he angry with her? Elizabeth tried to tell herself that she was misreading him again. She had made a vow not to rush to judgment, and so she would not. Instead, she would simply ask.

"Have I offended you, sir?"

Mr. Darcy was taken aback. "Of course not, Miss Elizabeth. I am sure that whatever reason you have for returning to your family, it is an excellent one. I only hope it is not because your injuries are worse than you believed."

Elizabeth worried her bottom lip for a moment. She had hoped to sort through it all with her family first, but there was nothing for it now. "I have not returned due to any physical ailment, sir."

Mr. Darcy pondered her reply for only a moment before he stood with a thunderous frown. She could see at once that he had correctly identified the problem.

"What is it, Darcy?" the colonel asked.

"*Who* is it, more like." Mr. Darcy took a step as though he wished to pace, but recalled himself and took his seat again.

The colonel was properly horrified. "She would not be so imprudent."

The expression on Mr. Darcy's countenance could only be called a pained smirk. "Would she not?"

"Elizabeth," her uncle said, rubbing his eyes, "please continue."

She related her part of the story without embellishment. The letter from the earl and the footmen's loose tongues. The way Lady Catherine had forced her way into the parsonage without being invited, how she had stood in the doorway of the Collinses' dining room, interrupting their meal and ordering that Elizabeth be thrown out into the night. The more she related, the grimmer the expressions of her uncle and Mr. Darcy became. Elizabeth skipped past some of the worst details because she was becoming quite anxious for them both.

"Charlotte mistook the time of the post," she said weakly, coming to the end of her tale. "And obviously, I could not return to the parsonage. Mr. Anders was kind enough to offer me the use of Mr. Darcy's carriage at Mrs. Collins's request." She peeked up at Mr. Darcy. "I would not have accepted had I any other choice."

Jane would not look at her. They both knew that Charlotte was meticulous; she would not have unintentionally mistaken the schedule of the post carriage. Fortunately, no one else in the room knew Mrs. Collins well enough to suspect any other motive on her part.

Mr. Darcy stood, tugged at the hem of his waistcoat, and cleared his throat. "Mr. Gardiner, might I request a private audience with Miss Elizabeth?"

"I beg you would not," Elizabeth blurted out.

Mr. Darcy's countenance reddened. "Pardon me?"

"Elizabeth," her aunt said quietly, "we cannot contain this. Even now the neighbours will be talking of Mr. Darcy's carriage. If Mrs. Collins is correct, Lady Catherine has already informed her acquaintances that you threw yourself at Mr. Darcy when he is the rightful property of her daughter."

"That is not true," Colonel Fitzwilliam said firmly. "About my cousin Miss de Bourgh."

Aunt Gardiner lifted an eyebrow at him, and the colonel hastened to add, "Nor the part about the compromise, of course."

"I know," Elizabeth interjected. "At least about the engagement being a wish and not a fact. Agnes told me."

"Agnes had much to say." Aunt Gardiner was now observing Elizabeth with her keen eye. "I might wonder what questions you were asking?"

"She did not require much prompting," Elizabeth replied. She shifted, wishing to stand, and winced at her body's protests.

Jane stood and left the room.

"Mr. Darcy, I will be plain. I know you do not wish to marry me."

He appeared confused.

"I am not so stubborn as to say we may not yet be *required* to wed," she added before her aunt could speak again. "Only that we need not act this very minute. Might we not wait a day or two? Perhaps a young lady will walk into a society ball in a soaked gown or the heir to a dukedom will elope with a milkmaid, and all this nonsense will be forgot?"

Jane reappeared with some ice in a basin. She set it down and wrapped the pieces in a cloth before applying it to Elizabeth's foot.

Elizabeth thanked her sister and attempted to banish her embarrassment. She felt at a terrible disadvantage, speaking with Mr. Darcy with one leg propped up before her like an invalid. However, the ice did help.

"Waiting a short time will not cost me anything," Mr. Darcy said slowly. "However, it may cost you a great deal. I would not have you punished for helping me, Miss Elizabeth."

"Perhaps we ought to give Elizabeth and Mr. Darcy a moment to speak with one another." Aunt Gardiner sent a silent but stern warning to her husband. Colonel Fitzwilliam waited for Mr. Darcy's quick nod, and then walked out with Jane by his side.

Mr. Gardiner was the last to leave, and he very purposefully left the door ajar.

Once they were alone, Elizabeth gestured that he ought to sit in the chair nearest her. When he was settled, she said, "I understand there is a risk. But you see, Mr. Darcy, I have always hoped to marry where there is a mutual sense of respect and admiration."

"But I do admire and respect you, Miss Elizabeth."

"I am very flattered. But such feelings, on their own, will not survive future marital disappointments." Elizabeth had only to observe her parents for evidence of that. Mr. Darcy began to protest, and she held up a hand. "Regardless, you forget that *your* respect and admiration are not the only ones at issue."

He was clearly quite surprised at her revelation. "I had thought we were friendly acquaintances at least, though I admit I did all I could to prevent you from detecting any special preference on my part. You truly do not feel those things for me?"

"Special preference?"

"Of course. You did not notice? I asked you to dance several times."

As though she would suspect an attachment based upon an insult for which he had not apologised and a few requests to dance! Elizabeth silently reined in her temper, reciting all the good deeds Mr. Darcy had performed on her behalf in the past two days before venturing to speak again. He *had* done well. He deserved an explanation.

"You have only yourself to blame, sir."

"I am not sure what you mean."

"Before we were even introduced, you called me tolerable but not handsome in a way that would tempt you. As such, you could not be persuaded to acknowledge me, not even for a dance. Is it any wonder I did not believe your subsequent requests to be in earnest?"

His mouth opened as though he would answer her, but then he closed it again.

"And it was not only the assembly where you derided my looks. I am aware that you and your friends, other than Mr. Bingley, enjoyed many clever insults about my appearance for some weeks after." She stared at him in challenge. "Am I wrong?"

"I . . ." He faltered to a stop.

Elizabeth knew Mr. Darcy had looked at her without admiration at the assembly, and when they next met, he looked at her only to criticise. She had been told that he spent the first few weeks of his time at Netherfield making it clear to Miss Bingley and the Hursts that Elizabeth had hardly a good feature in her face. It had been a source of anger and embarrassment for her, and she had refused to dance with him twice, not believing his offers sincere.

She was satisfied when Mr. Darcy shook his head to indicate that she was not wrong. At least she could be sure that he was not a liar. "You really ought to be more careful around servants you do not know, sir."

Mr. Darcy's sigh was profound, and she almost felt sorry for him.

"The notion of admiration, then, we may safely set aside. And given your own behaviour in the autumn, can you claim that you would respect me as your wife? I readily admit that my perception of you is vastly improved over the past two days, but that is two days, sir, out of several months that we have known one another. Remember, if you will, that marrying me would require being in company with my family from time to time. Not only Jane and the Gardiners, but my entire family."

"I do recall, madam."

"I do not think you would wish that."

His expression creased. "You must confess that your mother and younger sisters have demonstrated a severe lack of propriety."

"I do not always like my family, Mr. Darcy," she said softly, "but I do love them. A sentiment with which I might suggest you are familiar."

He stared at her, nonplussed.

"Lady Catherine?"

Mr. Darcy grunted. "A hit, a very palpable hit."

"A quote from *Hamlet*. Well done, Mr. Darcy. Perhaps we do have a love of Shakespeare in common, though I prefer the comedies to the tragedies."

"I suspected as much. You dearly love to laugh."

She offered him a little smile and a tight shake of her head. "You remember that silly statement?"

"There is very little about you that I do not remember, Miss Elizabeth."

Mr. Darcy spoke with sincerity and warmth, and Elizabeth did not know what to make of the little flutter it caused in her heart. She decided not to tease him about forgetting his initial insult of her.

"Miss Elizabeth," he said at last. "I must ask. You know that it is very probable we will be required to wed? For your reputation even more than my own."

"I am not ready to accept that, Mr. Darcy. For though I believe that you are, in essentials, a good man, I cannot believe you particularly enamoured of me."

He sputtered, but she would not allow him to deny it.

"You may never admire me—that may be too much to hope—but I begin to believe that respect may be possible. I ask for a few more days, no more than a week, before we determine how to proceed. It is not so very much, is it?"

"I suppose not." He clasped his hands together before him. "Before we end this tête-à-tête, however, I should like to say something."

"Mr. Darcy . . ." she protested quietly, not at all sure what that would accomplish.

"Miss Elizabeth," he said solemnly, "please. You have had your say. Am not I entitled to mine?"

Elizabeth took a deep breath. "Of course," she said politely.

Chapter Eleven

Darcy stood and took a circuit around the room, his mind a whirl of conflicting thoughts. When he had first seen Miss Elizabeth being assisted by her aunt and sister, it was all he could do not to sweep her into his arms himself, so powerful was his need to care for her.

That was the problem, was it not? She was not his to care for. Not yet.

Darcy had done his work too well in Hertfordshire. He had meant only to prevent raising Miss Elizabeth's expectations, but he had clearly shot wide of the mark and persuaded her that he did not care for her at all. He knew how well he had buried his admiration—had he been handed a shovel, he could not have dug a deeper hole.

Darcy had certainly disliked being in Hertfordshire, and he had resented the power Miss Elizabeth held over him, a power he now realised she had no idea she possessed.

Compromise, rumour, innuendo—they no longer mattered. He had made his decision the moment he saw her being helped inside her uncle's house. He *wanted* to marry her, could no longer think of marrying any other woman. That should have been the end of it.

Was this not the conceit of which his cousin had accused him? He had thought only his mind needed to be settled on the matter. He had assumed that given the circumstances, Miss Elizabeth would be anxious to accept his hand. Yet she had been given neither the time nor any reason to develop similar feelings for him, and no matter their predicament, she would not accept a man she was unsure of.

Miss Elizabeth's fortune and connections might be trifling, but her sterling character was itself a rare, precious treasure. Darcy longed for the time to court her properly, to show her the man he truly was, to help her return his own ardent feelings.

Time, however, was against them.

He heard his father's admonition in his head. "Patience, Fitzwilliam. Most problems can be resolved if you take them one step at a time."

Very well. She had admitted to the possibility of respect. It was a start.

He sat again beside her. Her complexion was pale, her features drawn. "I fear this has been a very trying time for you."

"And for you," she replied, and he acknowledged that it was so.

"Miss Elizabeth," he said gravely, "I am aware that I did not comport myself well in Hertfordshire, and it has resulted in a serious misunderstanding between us."

"I did not misunderstand."

"You did, because I made quite sure that you would."

"Please, Mr. Darcy," she said tiredly, "it has been a very long day. May we dispense with the riddles?"

He almost reached for her hand but stopped himself before she noticed.

"I *did* think myself clever, deriding you and your neighbours. It was such a spur to my genius to have Miss Bingley encouraging me to greater and greater spite." He ran one hand through his hair. "It was not gentlemanly at all, and I am ashamed of myself. But I must say that you were not really the subject of my ire."

"Who *was*, sir, if not those whom you insulted so freely?"

The name ground itself out from between his teeth. "Wickham."

She tipped her head and met his gaze, a bit of spark in her dark eyes. *She is curious,* he thought with satisfaction.

"And why is that, Mr. Darcy?"

More than a half year later, the wounds from Ramsgate were healing, and Darcy could see things more rationally. It was not only a physical longing he felt for Miss Elizabeth. She wanted a man who admired and respected her? He already did. In fact, he loved her. But she was not sure of him. He would have to tell her all.

"Because,"—he lowered his voice although they were sitting so close together—"only weeks before my arrival at Netherfield, he attempted to elope with my sister." He paused. "She was only fifteen at the time, which must be her excuse."

Miss Elizabeth gasped softly. Darcy swallowed and moved his gaze away from her lips. He must focus on his explanation, not act like a dog in heat.

"I was in a foul temper," he admitted, "and here were a group of people I considered beneath me and whom I should never see again. Perhaps they were gentry, but to my mind, they were no better than Wickham, speaking of my income before I had taken three steps inside the room. All looking for what they could get and caring not at all for me or mine."

"You were bitter."

"I was."

"A bitterness like that might well do you more harm than him."

He hesitated, nodded, and began again. "An angry man is seldom a wise one."

"True."

He allowed himself a little smile. "If you would allow me . . . I should like to tell you a secret, though you must promise to keep it."

"A secret greater than the one you have just related?"

"With so many sisters yourself, you would never relate a tale that might injure mine. I know your character well enough to be sure of that."

Miss Elizabeth nodded. "Thank you for the compliment and your trust. As for what you wish to tell me, I do enjoy a good secret, Mr. Darcy."

Darcy hated laying himself bare, and so he never did. He hoped that Miss Elizabeth would not think less of him for it, but to prove he thought well of her, some sacrifice would be required. He leaned forward just a bit. "I do not speak a great deal in company, but it does not follow that my feelings are shallow."

Miss Elizabeth watched him closely but did not speak.

"When I was a boy, my father was in fact concerned that my emotions would get the better of me one day. He did not want me to be impulsive, to make a mistake with Pemberley."

"Your estate."

"My family's estate, yes. A significant portion of my education was therefore focused on self-control."

"You learned that lesson perhaps too well, Mr. Darcy. Is the mask you wear in company the result of your training?"

"Mask?" He blinked. It was a rather apt description, and he pinched the bridge of his nose. "I suppose."

Miss Elizabeth nodded solemnly. "Mr. Wickham has a mask of his own that he wears, but I do not believe he learned it from your father."

"Perhaps he did, in a sense. My father never did discern what he was. He sent Wickham to school and did everything he could to ease Wickham's way. He instructed me to help settle Wickham in a profession and left him a thousand pounds. Yet . . ."

"Yet here he is, not much younger than you, and all he has done is attempt to injure your sister, for her fortune, I expect?"

Darcy nodded.

"Then, failing in that endeavour and all his own money spent, he has joined the militia." She shook her head. "And then he attempted to injure you. Yet until the night at the theatre, I believed him the wronged party."

Darcy squeezed his hands together. "He fooled my father, Miss Elizabeth. I would not have you blame yourself for believing Mr. Wickham, too." He glanced away. "I should add that he had more than the bequest. He was paid three thousand pounds for a living which was left to him on the condition he take orders, a condition he had not met. And when the money was gone, he returned to demand the living he had signed away."

Miss Elizabeth frowned.

"George Wickham is not a man I recommend anyone trust. He is a scoundrel who lives off the goodwill and hard work of others without returning anything of value himself."

"He is a very handsome man," she said, musing.

Darcy's heart sank. "He has not imposed himself . . ."

Her expression cleared. "Oh heavens, no. He is engaged, in fact, to a young Miss King who has recently come into an inheritance."

"Of course he is."

"I was merely ruminating. Mr. Wickham and Jane are possibly the most beautiful people I have ever met."

"Thank you," he said drily.

This surprised her enough that she chuckled, and her eyes sparkled. "You are not so bad-looking yourself, you know, when you smile."

He shook his head at her but could not resist offering her one.

"There," she said, satisfied. "Just like that."

"I shall endeavour to smile more, if it pleases you."

Her brows pinched together in confusion. "I believe one typically smiles because something has pleased *him*."

"Perhaps," he said. "It was not the fashion in my home."

She stared at him for a moment, a flash of sympathy offering him hope. "I freely admit that Jane is five times as pretty as the rest of us. The difference is that my sister's beauty is not only in her face and figure but in her very being. Mr. Wickham trades on his good looks to hide a blackened soul." Softly, she added, "And you hide *yourself*."

"Your sister is a lovely woman," he agreed, uncomfortable with her assessment.

She wrinkled her little nose at him, and he felt the corners of his mouth tug up.

"It is more than that. Jane may be too willing to forgive or excuse, but she does not give her heart away easily. When she does, it is without reservation."

Darcy was quiet.

"Do you know, she has convinced herself that she must have been entirely mistaken in Mr. Bingley's regard? That he simply did not realise he was raising her expectations?"

Darcy could not pretend he did not glean her meaning. "I did not believe your sister had any special regard for him."

Miss Elizabeth closed her eyes. "A woman is censured if she demonstrates her feelings before the man confesses his own. Jane is a very proper woman, sir."

So was Miss Elizabeth. He must take the lead if he were to succeed in winning her.

"I might even say," Miss Elizabeth added, "that my sister has perhaps too much self-control. Not unlike you?"

Touché. "I shall inform Bingley that your sister is in town. I was already planning to do so."

She met his eye. "I ask for nothing more. Mr. Bingley must come to Jane on his own if he wishes to make amends, and of course, he must first carefully consider the potential for scandal. If that will frighten him off, it is better that he not come at all."

Darcy could only agree. To visit Miss Bennet without any intentions of making an offer now—that would be more than ungentlemanly, it would be cruel.

"I will say only one thing more. Should he decide to visit, he ought to arrange it through my uncle. Jane deserves time to compose herself."

She was as fiercely protective of her sister as he was his own. "I have always admired your willingness to come to your sister's aid, Miss Elizabeth."

"Thank you, Mr. Darcy."

He heard stirring in the hallway and stood. "May I propose a compromise, madam?"

"A compromise?" One side of Miss Elizabeth's mouth lifted into a half-smile. "I believe we have already accomplished that, sir."

This drew a quiet laugh from him. "We have met three times now without intention. Avoiding one another seems a hopeless business." He felt as mischievous as he had as a boy when he added, "My cousin calls it fate."

"Indeed?" Miss Elizabeth responded in kind. "Is the colonel a reader of many romantic novels, then? As the heroine of this little tale, must I be abducted and tossed in the box of a carriage to reach my happy end? For I must tell you, I would find that very uncomfortable."

She was everything delightful.

"I have a less drastic method in mind, Miss Elizabeth. Should we instead simply plan to be seen together as members of a larger party? It might offer an alternative explanation as to why we were together at the theatre."

"It would not, unfortunately, explain my hold on your cravat, nor how we came to fall to the ground."

"Your hold may be denied as rumour, and the rest by the mob fleeing what they believed was a fire. You were there with your family, hardly a promising opportunity for an illicit rendezvous."

"You would be seen in public with my uncle the tradesman?" Her words were challenging.

"Your uncle is the owner of a number of establishments, is not that the case?"

"It is."

"Bingley still derives income from his father's companies, though he is not directly involved in their operation, and as you know, I consider him a particular friend."

"My uncle *is* still directly involved in the management of his businesses, however. When I was a child, he even took me to see his Flemish workers and their silkworms, so I would know where the material for my mother's ballgowns came from. It is one of my fondest memories."

Darcy relished the thought of a young Elizabeth being taken on such an outing. "Did Miss Bennet accompany you?"

"Oh no," Miss Elizabeth replied merrily. "Other than children, Jane does not like things that crawl."

Miss Elizabeth might love her family at Longbourn, but she also admired and respected the Gardiners, and from what he had seen, they were estimable people. "I would be pleased to be seen in company with them."

Miss Elizabeth did not appear persuaded, but Darcy was resolute. He would be a fool to allow this opportunity to pass him by. Having now decided that his life would be an immeasurably happier one with her in it, and that he would bear any consequences their alliance might bring, he was determined to win her heart and then her hand.

"May I have your answer, madam?"

Her expression cleared. "Very well. The final decision must rest with my uncle and aunt, but I am amenable."

"What do you mean?" Uncle Gardiner asked warily.

"You know," Colonel Fitzwilliam muttered, "that might just work."

"One wrong move," Aunt Gardiner warned, "and this entire house of cards will come tumbling down."

"I understand there is a risk we shall make things worse," Mr. Darcy said quietly, his expression again unyielding, "but I do not believe we will. Lord and Lady Matlock may be counted upon. They will be displeased with Lady Catherine for dragging others into what they view as family business."

Colonel Fitzwilliam nodded.

"I am not sure what having Elizabeth seen with the man who is said to have compromised her will do for her." Uncle Gardiner crossed his arms over his chest.

"She will not be with me alone," Mr. Darcy said. "You will all be with us. A family party. Even Lord and Lady Matlock shall join us once I explain the situation to them."

Aunt Gardiner's expression was thoughtful.

"Think like a gossip, Mr. Gardiner," Colonel Fitzwilliam added. "What is there to whisper about when nothing is being kept secret? Would a business connection between yourself and my cousin not be a more likely explanation for why he and Miss Elizabeth were together at the theatre and why she was so willing to help him?"

Jane shook her head. "It might also suggest that a marriage is imminent, and when it does not take place, Lizzy will be named a jilt."

"We will make sure that does not happen."

"How?"

"Because, Miss Bennet," Mr. Darcy said firmly, "if it becomes necessary, I will make Miss Elizabeth an offer of my hand. The only question, truly, is whether she will accept it."

"I am the one who requested more time, Jane," Elizabeth said softly.

"Elizabeth?" Aunt Gardiner asked. "How do you feel about Mr. Darcy's strategy?"

"I suppose I shall have to pretend to be pleased with Mr. Darcy's presence?" she asked pertly, arching one brow at the man.

"Elizabeth!" her aunt cried warningly.

He did not smile, but his eyes were bright. "As difficult as that must be for you, Miss Elizabeth, I fear it will be necessary."

Mr. Darcy had a sense of humour, which boded well. Elizabeth sighed dramatically. "I suppose I can pretend I am Lydia and draw upon my acting skills."

Her aunt shared a look with her uncle. The way they spoke without words warmed her heart.

Would she ever be able to have that sort of marriage with Mr. Darcy?

"Very well," her uncle said. "We shall play this out with the understanding that if it becomes necessary, Mr. Darcy will make an honourable offer. Elizabeth will be mending for a few days. I do not want her walking on that ankle again until it is sound."

"Agreed."

"Perhaps . . ." Jane said, then stopped herself to look around the room.

"Yes, dear?" Aunt Gardiner asked.

"Perhaps it would not be so obvious if Mr. Darcy was seen primarily in the company of my uncle and his friends, and then, occasionally, with the rest of us."

Mr. Darcy frowned at that, but Elizabeth turned a bright smile on her sister.

"An excellent suggestion, Jane," Aunt Gardiner said.

"Perhaps you gentlemen might be so good as to call upon me at my office?" Uncle Gardiner asked. "I am well-known here, and it would be a friendlier way to begin. I suspect the reaction in your neighbourhood will be more . . ."

"Venomous?" Colonel Fitzwilliam supplied teasingly. "You are not wrong."

Elizabeth was watching Mr. Darcy. That her uncle had surprised him was certain, but he had recovered quickly. "I shall. Would tomorrow be convenient?"

"We can put it about that you are considering investing."

"Will that work, dear?" Aunt Gardiner inquired mildly.

Mr. Gardiner wagged his head thoughtfully. "With a man of Mr. Darcy's wealth, I believe it will."

"Is there a reason such an explanation might not be accepted, Mr. Gardiner?"

"Not as such, Mr. Darcy. It is well-known that I do not take on investors. Or at least, I never have."

"Surely your businesses might expand with the infusion of capital," the colonel said, interested.

"And that way many businesses have been lost. No, I prefer to answer only to myself for the good of my business and my workers. Someday I may decide to scale up the enterprises, but I will never open the door to just anyone. For now, I wish to see how things on the continent will end."

"Wise. I believe many will be ruined when those markets open to trade again," Mr. Darcy said. "The corn prices alone . . ."

"I do not traffic in corn, but I see we will not lack for topics of discussion," her uncle said. He rang the bell, and Vaz appeared. Uncle Gardiner nodded in Elizabeth's direction, and the man nodded back.

Jane removed what remained of the ice from Elizabeth's ankle, placing it and the cloths into a basin. Then she pulled Elizabeth's skirts down so that they completely covered her before her uncle helped her to stand.

Elizabeth's ankle was feeling better, but the proof would be whether she could walk on it in the morning. "You have all given me a great deal to ponder. I thank you for your efforts on my behalf, Mr. Darcy," Elizabeth said, badly needing to be alone for a time.

"Take care, Miss Elizabeth," Mr. Darcy said, bowing over her hand and offering a tiny smile that only she could see. "I look forward to meeting again."

He and the colonel made their way out. At least she would not be embarrassed by having them witness Vaz carrying her above stairs.

When Elizabeth had been delivered to her room and awaited a maid to assist her, all she could think about was the kind, flawed, gentlemanly, confounding Mr. Darcy.

Chapter Twelve

The Darcy carriage, handsome and easily identifiable, made its way directly from Gracechurch Street to his townhouse. There was little use in trying to hide the connection now.

"Have you any idea where Mrs. Younge resides?" Fitzwilliam asked as Anders guided them around a ragman's wagon.

Darcy closed the window. "She removed to a house in Southwark."

"Near the Marshalsea. Appropriate."

"I shall send out a man on the morrow to find the exact direction."

"Very well," Fitzwilliam replied. "In the meantime, I shall keep an ear to the ground for Wickham."

Darcy nodded. "I will begin visiting Mr. Gardiner tomorrow as well. I am rather intrigued with his business."

"Businesses," Fitzwilliam said with a smirk. "I had a better look at those paintings in the entry hall on our way out. An Adam Buck, and another painting that looked very like Dovedale. I wonder if it might have been by Wright."

"Wright of Derby?"

"It looks very like."

"Mr. Gardiner's businesses," Darcy said, with an emphasis on the plural, "must be doing rather well."

"Perhaps that is why Miss Elizabeth feels at liberty to refuse you."

"She did not refuse me. She prevented me from offering."

Fitzwilliam sat back against the squabs and crossed his arms over his chest. "Perhaps she is not so intelligent as you believe."

He might have been relieved to think so, not so long ago. Now, the insult fired his temper. "Miss Elizabeth Bennet knows me well enough to know she would not choose me for her husband."

"She is dissembling."

"Fitzwilliam," Darcy nearly growled.

"What could you possibly have done that made any reasonable woman turn down your offer?"

"She did *not* refuse my offer," Darcy repeated. "I have not yet made one."

"Hoping to increase your love by suspense? A very dangerous game to play for a woman in her situation."

"Elizabeth is *in* this situation because of me and, may I remind you, because of *you*. Most of all, she is in trouble because of that damned scoundrel Wickham. Finally, despite how I treated her in Hertfordshire, she put her own safety at risk to save me. I will not hear you, or anyone else, speak ill of her."

Fitzwilliam's smile was wide and smug.

Damn him.

"Elizabeth, is it?" his cousin said languidly.

"Cousin . . ." Darcy said slowly.

"Yes?"

"As you will hound me until I capitulate, I shall save us both the aggravation. Between us?"

Fitzwilliam nodded. "My word."

"I would beg your father to procure a special license for me this very hour if I thought she would say yes. But I have been unkind, superior, ungentlemanly, and she is rightfully leery of my ability to be a good husband to her."

Fitzwilliam tipped his head to one side. "What, exactly, did you *do* when you were with Bingley in the countryside?"

The carriage pulled up outside the townhouse, and Darcy sighed. "Let us have dinner with Georgiana. When she retires, we can adjourn to my study, and I will tell you everything."

"Is this a conversation that is going to require brandy, or will wine suffice?"

"Brandy," Darcy said. "Definitely brandy."

"*Darcy*," his cousin groaned.

After Elizabeth had assured her family that she was not hungry and they need not wait on her to serve their dinner, a maid helped her bathe and change. Her bruised face was tended to, and she was now sitting in bed, her injured foot now resting on a soft pillow, left to contemplate all that had happened.

Eventually, Jane came in to say good night. Elizabeth patted one side of the bed and Jane sat next to her.

"What is Mr. Darcy about, Jane?"

"I am not privy to Mr. Darcy's thoughts, Lizzy."

"Were it not for your suggestion that he spend most of his time with Uncle Gardiner, we would be forced to the altar in a trice. What can he be thinking?"

"My clever sister," Jane said, laying her hand over Elizabeth's, "can you not guess?"

Elizabeth closed her eyes. What Jane suggested was only due to her loving heart. "I cannot. I am so tired, Jane."

"And in some pain, I fear."

"That as well, though not being in a carriage is an improvement."

"I will have some willow bark tea brought up. It should ease you enough to sleep."

Jane sat up, but Elizabeth opened her eyes and grabbed her sister's hand. "Do not go, Jane."

Jane settled back on the pillows.

"Does he see a marriage as inevitable and wish to ease our way?"

"That is possible," Jane replied.

Elizabeth hoped not. It would be a sad fate indeed to have escaped one marriage of convenience for another, even if Mr. Darcy was a far superior man to Mr. Collins. "But you do not think it likely."

"Again, Lizzy, I cannot say what Mr. Darcy intends. I will tell you what I have observed, if you like."

Elizabeth sighed, relieved. "Please do."

Jane paused to gather her thoughts. "When we were in Hertfordshire, I was surprised by him. You had told us of his insult, yet the very next time we met in company, his eyes followed you. Then *he* began to follow you. Do you not remember the evening at Lucas

Lodge? Even Mr. Bingley remarked upon how his friend listened to you and ignored everyone else."

"To find fault," Elizabeth said weakly, no longer believing it.

"He asked you to dance, and you declined."

"Mr. Darcy was pressed into asking."

"You mentioned that he asked you to dance a reel at Netherfield. Was he being coerced then?"

Elizabeth said, without conviction, "He was mocking . . ."

"Then he requested your hand at the ball when he danced with no one else outside his own party. Thank goodness you accepted him then."

"I could not think of anything to say that would put him off."

Jane laughed gently. "Surely not. The witty Elizabeth Bennet, at a loss for words?"

"You are not funny."

"No, but you are." Jane shook her head. "Truly, I did not know what to make of it then, but after witnessing Mr. Darcy's gallantry towards you over the past few days . . . I believe he was interested in you even in Hertfordshire, Lizzy. But after he had insulted you, how could he make the first approach?"

This was a very kind interpretation. Elizabeth recalled how Mr. Darcy had eavesdropped on all her conversations at Lucas Lodge and how she had made sure he knew he had been caught out. Perhaps he had not been meaning to judge and insult her at every turn; she may have been mistaken there. But neither had he sought to recommend himself, nor did she believe he had been attempting to further their acquaintance.

"If he had any interest in me at all, he fought against it."

Jane sighed. "As many men do, I am told."

"Oh, Jane, I did not mean to imply . . ."

Her sister waved the apology away. "You did not, Lizzy. Will you hear me?"

"I will."

"Mr. Bingley paid me a great deal of attention before he had decided what his intentions were, and then he disappeared. Mr. Darcy cared for you just as much but concealed those feelings so as not to raise your expectations."

Elizabeth considered that.

"Now that he *has* decided to pursue you, I believe he will not shrink from showing you every courtesy." She patted Elizabeth's hand. "Of the two approaches, I know which I prefer."

Elizabeth did have a few quibbles with Jane's view of things, but she could not deny the truth of her conclusion. "Has Mr. Darcy decided, though? Or have recent events made that decision for him?"

"You know as well as I that he could offer to settle the matter without marriage."

She had said as much herself. "That is true." She was quiet for a moment. "Jane," she asked anxiously, "no one has written Mamma or Papa to mention this debacle, have they?"

"Not yet, but my uncle will write Papa, I am sure."

"Good. Then we shall have at least a month before uncle receives a reply."

"Lizzy."

Elizabeth closed her eyes. "As kind as Sir William has been, he is not discreet. Even if he means to defend me, in a week he will be home and Lady Lucas will know it all. She will tell Mamma, and then everyone we have ever met will know that Lady Catherine threw me out of the parsonage because she thought I was trying to compromise Mr. Darcy. Mamma will be . . . I cannot go back to Longbourn just now."

Her sister's voice was very soft. "I do not believe Uncle Gardiner will be sending you home to Longbourn, Lizzy."

"That is a relief." Mamma would fly into hysterics if she knew what had happened to Elizabeth these past days, and Papa would think it all great sport. One would berate her for her wild ways, and the other would laugh at her. Neither would be conducive to her peace of mind.

Mr. Darcy had not laughed when informed of Lady Catherine's fury. He had been offended on Elizabeth's behalf, every bit as much as Uncle Gardiner had been. She did not wish to admit to herself that it had made her feel protected. Valued.

"Mamma and Papa love us, Lizzy."

"Not as they should, Jane. Mamma only sees us as reflections of herself. When she was angry at Mr. Darcy for insulting me, she was angry because he had dared to insult one of her daughters, not because he had hurt me."

Jane plucked lightly at Elizabeth's sleeve. "You laughed, Lizzy. Were you hurt?"

"A little, perhaps. Of course, being the less handsome second sister has required that I become more inured to such complaints."

"Oh, Lizzy," Jane remonstrated. "You are very pretty, as you well know."

"I am not hurt now," Lizzy said. "Only confused."

"About Mr. Darcy?"

"Yes."

"He must be in love with you, I think."

"This is my quandary, Jane. How *can* he be in love when he hardly knows me? Mr. Darcy's willingness to wed, if indeed he is truly willing, is not proof against his regret when he wakes one morning and determines that he has been hasty and that I am not, in fact, his equal. He *says* he respects and admires me, but I am afraid . . ."

"That you will have a marriage like our parents?"

Elizabeth looked away and nodded.

She heard her sister sigh softly. "I share your fear. But while I find Mr. Darcy every bit as clever as Papa, he is not given to impulsive decisions."

"He was on his way to Kent, Jane. His decision to leave town for the country was likely an impulsive one."

"His family, like yours, most likely thought it best to allow time for the rumours to die away. And yet, when he saw you in need, he did not shun you as he might have. As he *ought* to have, if indeed he did not wish his name connected with yours. Instead, he acted every bit the gentleman."

Not every bit. She shivered a little as she remembered his hands around her waist, lifting her as though she weighed nothing at all. But how could she be sure that this was not the sort of shallow attraction that had led her parents to marry?

"It is a wonder either you or I wish to wed at all," Elizabeth said at last. "Only Uncle Gardiner has managed any kind of happiness for himself." She worried her bottom lip before pushing the conversation in another direction. "Jane, if Mr. Bingley returned now, would you allow him to call?"

This was sudden indeed, and Jane was quiet for a moment. "Why do you ask?"

"Only that if Mr. Darcy is to be in our company . . ."

There was a soft knock, and Aunt Gardiner opened the door when Elizabeth bade her enter.

Jane was still answering Elizabeth's question. "So much has happened today, I failed to consider that, but surely Mr. Bingley and I shall not often be in company. If we are, I shall have my family around me."

"I would not wish to discomfit you."

"Lizzy," Jane said with a sigh. "Mr. Bingley made me no promises. I can assure you now that while it may be awkward at first, I shall be well."

"Oh Jane." Elizabeth pulled herself up, and Aunt Gardiner immediately adjusted the pillow under her foot.

"These are important questions, Jane," their aunt said. "You should consider them."

"Aunt, my hopes are firmly fixed on Lizzy." Jane smiled and took Elizabeth's hands. "I am your champion in this, and I do believe that Mr. Darcy would make you a very good husband."

"If only I could be sure *why*, after all his disdain when he was at Netherfield, Mr. Darcy has changed his mind."

"Lizzy, do not be obtuse," Jane said with a little laugh. "He has not changed his mind about you, only what he ought to do about it. As much as you do not wish to own it, you saved him in the theatre." There was a bit of sarcasm in Jane's voice as she added, "Is it not possible he *finally* admitted to himself that you were a woman worthy of his great name?"

Aunt Gardiner chuckled.

"Jane!" Elizabeth exclaimed cheerfully. "That was as pert a thing as I have ever heard you say. Well done!" She laid her head on her sister's shoulder.

"I may not often say such things, dearest. It does not mean I do not think them." Jane kissed the top of Lizzy's head and then rose, casting a glance at Aunt Gardiner. "I will ring for the tea."

"Lizzy," Aunt Gardiner said. "It could not have been easy to speak your mind when the drawing room was so crowded. I should like to know your thoughts now so I will know how to proceed."

"What do you mean, Aunt?"

"If you truly wish to spend time with Mr. Darcy, I shall do everything in my power to ease your way. The same is true if you do not wish it. Only you must tell me which way I am to direct my efforts."

It was too much. She did not wish to speak of this any more tonight. "I hardly know."

"When you do—and Lizzy, you must give serious thought to it while you are recuperating—I must insist that you inform me at once."

Elizabeth took a deep breath. "I shall, Aunt Gardiner."

Her aunt patted her cheek and said good night to her nieces before heading to her own bed.

After ensuring Elizabeth had drunk two cups of the bitter brew, Jane kissed the top of her sister's head and retired to her own chamber. As tired as she was, Elizabeth could not sleep while her thoughts were in such a tangle.

After all the inhabitants of the house had settled for the night and a deep quiet descended, Elizabeth sank into her pillows. The tea was beginning to work and rather than focusing on her discomfort, she could turn her weary mind to the thorny problem of Mr. Darcy.

Jane's words rang in her ears. *He has not changed his mind about you, only what he ought to do about it*. Had not Charlotte implied the same? She put aside the first few weeks of their acquaintance and attempted to view their other interactions as Charlotte and Jane had.

Mr. Darcy had argued with her at Netherfield, but as she turned each exchange over in her mind, she realised that, seen in another light, it was a compliment to her; he respected her intelligence enough to engage her in debate.

He had stared at her, his looks heated and intense, but what she had mistaken for anger she now saw differently, as desire. She did not understand it, but she had seen it between engaged couples before. It unsettled her, but it did not make her afraid.

Despite leaving Hertfordshire and not returning, his stares today had been every bit as intense as they had been in the autumn. And the things he had said to her before he took his leave! Those were the most shocking of all. His feelings for her were strong. Constant.

This was a fine beginning. But could *she* care for *him*?

Finally, Elizabeth pondered everything Agnes had revealed about Mr. Darcy and reviewed his behaviour over the past few days. Agnes believed him a responsible, fair, kind man, and had not Elizabeth seen it herself? Fine words were one thing, but he had cared for the safety of her person and her reputation even when it put his own at risk. For a brief moment when she was being assisted to the drawing room today, his gaze had been so anxious, so concerned, she thought he might actually pick her up and transport her to the nearest settee. What a scandal *that* would have been.

Elizabeth remembered the feel of his hands on her waist, of his gentle touch on her face, and she almost wished he had done it.

There, in the dark, her cheeks warmed with what must be a spectacular blush.

"Oh," she whispered, covering her face with her hands. "I have strong feelings for him, too."

Chapter Thirteen

Darcy stood on the corner nearest the Hursts' home on Grosvenor Street, where Bingley stayed with Miss Bingley and the Hursts when in town. Fitzwilliam waited in the carriage, for Darcy intended only to leave his card and ask his friend to meet him elsewhere. He did not wish to have a conversation about Miss Jane Bennet in the same house as the women who had disparaged her.

He did not believe he deserved the facer Fitzwilliam had mentioned, not for offering his opinion—Darcy truly had not done so until Bingley inquired. However, that opinion had been wrong, and it was his obligation to inform his friend so. Where he truly deserved the set down was over his decision to keep Miss Bennet's presence in town from Bingley. That had been wrong, too, but not at all innocent. He had considered it a favour to Bingley but realised now that he had been treating his friend like a child and in consequence, as Miss Elizabeth had informed him, wounded Miss Bennet.

The butler answered, he was shown inside. Darcy handed over his card but was delayed by the sound of Miss Bingley's voice.

"Mr. Darcy!" she cried, sweeping into the hall. "What a pleasant surprise! Do come in and visit a while."

A pleasant surprise? The woman ate gossip for breakfast. He had expected at least a show of feigned outrage on his behalf for what had happened at the theatre, accompanied by half a dozen hints that he ought to marry someone he already knew and trusted so he might not be forced to make an alliance elsewhere.

"I am afraid I cannot," he said brusquely, grateful that Fitzwilliam had remained outside. "I am only here to leave my card for your brother."

"Oh, Charles is somewhere about," she said warmly. "Do come inside while we find him. We have not seen you in an age." She gave orders to the footman.

"My carriage waits outside, Miss Bingley," he said. "Forgive me, I cannot remain. Please tell your brother . . ."

"Tell me what, Darcy?" Bingley asked as he strode into the hall. "Thank you, Caroline," he said. "I will see to Darcy."

Miss Bingley's lips pressed together, but she offered a curtsy. "I hope to see you again soon, sir. You must come for dinner."

"This is not your house, Caroline," Bingley said in a tone that was blunter than Darcy had ever heard him use. "Louisa does the inviting here." He took Darcy by the arm and pulled him into the library, a small but comfortable room.

"Bingley," Darcy said, "I was not prevaricating. My carriage is waiting. I have come solely to invite you to dine with me or to meet with me at the club. There is something I would speak to you about."

"Does it have anything to do with this?" Bingley slapped a copy of the *Examiner* against Darcy's chest. "I know you would not compromise a woman, Darcy, but what happened? And why are you not making this right?"

"I am in the process of making this right, as you say. It is the lady who delays."

Bingley looked him up and down, a small smile gracing his face. "The lady makes you dance to her tune, eh? Good for her, I say."

"I am not dancing to anyone's tune, Bingley."

Bingley was not interested in Darcy's protest. He glanced uneasily at the library door. "I suspect Caroline is trying to listen in." He sighed. "You have no idea the intrigues I have gone through to keep this from my sisters."

"My thanks, Bingley."

"I cannot hold out much longer."

"Why not come with me now and we can discuss it tonight over dinner? Fitzwilliam is with me and aware of the particulars."

"Excellent, Darcy," Bingley said, his expression both grim and flustered. "Just get me out of this house."

A few minutes later, Bingley opened the door to the carriage and climbed inside.

Fitzwilliam laughed heartily. "The two of you look like rats fleeing a sinking ship. Is it so bad inside?"

"Not yet," Darcy replied coolly, "for Bingley has been hiding the paper."

"Bingley has?" Fitzwilliam exclaimed, grinning at Darcy's friend. "I would not have thought you had it in you!"

"I am absolutely moving back to the hotel tomorrow, Darcy," Bingley said after giving Fitzwilliam a withering glare entirely unlike his normal self. "I am forever grateful you did not invite us to join you at the theatre."

"Your sister asked me so many times," Darcy said, shaking his head. "I am sorry, Bingley. You are always welcome, you know, but I cannot abide that sort of thing. An invitation is something you are offered, not something you request."

"Repeatedly," Fitzwilliam added.

"I am aware of my sister's failings, Darcy," Bingley said. "I am here, am I not?"

"Fair." Darcy frowned. "Before the end of the night, you will be aware of mine as well."

"That does not sound like the Darcy I know," Bingley said slowly. He held up the paper that was still in his possession. "Do not tell me there is any truth in this report?"

"Not much," Darcy said as they entered the house. "But enough." He signalled the butler to take the paper and leave it in his study.

It was a good thing Mrs. Doughty was always ready to feed extra guests, for Bingley's appetite was extraordinary.

"Mrs. Hurst's cook is not ill, I hope?" Fitzwilliam quipped near the end of their repast.

Bingley looked up and swallowed the bread in his mouth. "She is well. Why do you ask?"

Darcy and Fitzwilliam laughed together.

"You look half-starved," Fitzwilliam said when they were through.

"Shall we repair somewhere more private?" Darcy asked. He smirked at his friend. "Unless you intend to eat the table leg?"

"It is your own fault, Darcy," Bingley grumbled as they rose. "I have been so busy preventing callers and intercepting notes from Caroline's friends that I have not had time to eat. Not that I would have been able. Turns my stomach thinking about that poor woman. Caroline and her friends will find out who she is and take their pleasure in ruining her."

Darcy closed his eyes.

"About that, Bingley," he said, and told his friend the entire tale, from the incident at the theatre to Miss Elizabeth's defence of her sister's tender heart.

After the recitation concluded, Bingley sat silently, his complexion so dreadfully pale that Darcy was concerned he might cast up his accounts. Given the prodigious meal Bingley had just consumed, he was somewhat afraid for his rug.

Fortunately, Bingley only said, very quietly, "She cared for me?" He set his drink down. Darcy's stomach gave a twist of its own. "Yes."

"She cared for me, and I left without so much as a proper farewell." Bingley dropped his head in his hands. "I am a cad."

"You are not a cad," Darcy protested.

Bingley raised his head. "No? You told me she did not care for me and that if I returned, her mother would certainly force her to accept my hand. And I believed you. You, a man who knows less about a woman's heart than anyone I know."

Darcy felt that a trifle exaggerated, but the ridiculousness of his attempt to give Bingley direction in the matter did ring true. "I truly did believe it, Bingley."

"It does not follow that I ought to have accepted it." He stood and took a few steps towards Darcy, who stood as well. "If you ever again collude with my sisters against me, Darcy . . ." He took a steadying breath. "I will accept your good intentions as your excuse this once. Should you ever try to manage me in such a way again, this friendship will be over. Have I made myself plain?"

"You have."

Fitzwilliam crossed his arms over his chest. "And thus, a boy becomes a man."

Darcy and Bingley both spoke at the same time. "Shut up, Fitzwilliam."

Bingley picked up his glass and finished his brandy. "Now," he said sombrely, "what is Mr. Gardiner's direction, Darcy? For I must contact him at once."

Jane narrowly avoided the maid carrying the breakfast tray downstairs when she stepped inside Elizabeth's room and snapped the door shut. In her hand was a folded piece of paper.

"Jane?" Elizabeth asked, alarmed. "Whatever is the matter?"

Her sister met her eye. "Mr. Bingley has written to me."

"He *what*?" she asked furiously.

"Oh. No, Lizzy," Jane said, waving off her sister's agitation. "He sent Uncle Gardiner a letter and included this one for me, unsealed. Uncle read it first and has only just given it to me. I read a little, but . . ."

"Well, then," Elizabeth said, satisfied that Mr. Bingley had not neglected propriety. They had experienced quite enough of that this week. "What has the man to say for himself?"

"It is an apology, Lizzy, from beginning to end, and a request to call on me here in town."

"I thought you had only read a little?" Elizabeth teased.

"I can hardly take it in," Jane replied with a laugh that was both happy and bemused. "He says he never knew I was in town at all, that his sisters never told him."

"Which does not address his manner of leaving Netherfield without so much as a farewell to his neighbours."

"But he does address it. Listen—'I have formerly been in the habit of taking advice from those I assumed knew better, but that time is past. Through my own lack of fortitude, I have injured you, which is precisely what I sought to avoid by not returning to Netherfield.'" Jane looked up. "He said Mr. Darcy was concerned Mamma might force me to accept him when I did not wish it."

"Well," Elizabeth said, surprised. "That is very forthright. And does he blame Mr. Darcy?"

"If he had, I would not be so impressed with the letter as I am. He takes it all upon himself. 'It was my friend's place to offer his advice, but my own decision to accept it.'" Jane pressed the letter to her chest. "After all this time I had convinced myself that he did not care for me," she said softly. "It makes me so happy to hear him say that he did. That he does."

Elizabeth smiled. "I presume, then, that you will allow him to call?"

"Lizzy," Jane said suddenly, "did you do this?"

"I can hardly write Mr. Bingley's letters for him, Jane," she said lightly.

"*Lizzy.* Did you speak to Mr. Darcy about his friend?"

"I may have mentioned something."

"Had this not come to such a happy conclusion, I should be quite angry with you, sister."

Elizabeth took her sister's hand. "Then I shall simply rejoice that it has and wish you and Mr. Bingley very happy."

"We shall require a serious conversation or two before that comes to pass. But what of you and Mr. Darcy?"

She could not resist replying with a tease. "I wish us both very happy too—in our own separate ways."

Jane slapped playfully at her shoulder. "You really are incorrigible, Lizzy."

"One of the many reasons you love me."

"Yes," said Jane, sitting on the bed and enfolding Elizabeth in her embrace. "I do."

Chapter Fourteen

Despite Darcy's distaste for it, their visit to Mrs. Younge's house had gone rather well. She did not know where Wickham was, or if she did, she was not saying. However, Georgiana's former companion had mentioned the name of the lady she thought him to be courting—and Darcy had heard the name before.

"Do you know this Mrs. Franke?" Fitzwilliam asked as they climbed into yet another hackney.

"Not personally, but your mother does."

"I shall never know how you keep all those names in your head. I know the names of my men, but I spend a great deal of time with them."

Darcy shrugged. "I possess no great facility in charming speeches, as you do. If I cannot put others at ease in that way, at least I can recall their names."

Fitzwilliam offered him an approving look. "Agreed." He removed his hat and thumbed the brim. "Wickham is coming up in the world if he is targeting wealthy widows."

"I very much doubt it. A woman like Mrs. Franke is not so easily fooled as a fifteen-year-old girl who was fond of him as a child. She may purchase him a few baubles, but she will never relinquish any control over her wealth."

"Perhaps that is all he needs." Fitzwilliam stifled a yawn. "A few trinkets and a place to stay. I suppose we shall be paying my dear mother a visit?"

"I intend to ask her and your father to appear in public with a tradesman. As estimable as the Gardiners are, it is not a small favour I am requesting. We will return to the house to refresh ourselves and use my carriage."

"You are fastidious."

"I am strategic. In such matters as these, my uncle follows my aunt. I need her in a good mood, and she would roast me on a spit were I to arrive in anything less than the best I possess."

"Although she would not mind if your coach was red or yellow instead of black."

"Impractical. Black shows the dirt less."

Fitzwilliam laughed. "You know my mother is possibly the least practical woman in all of England when it comes to appearances. She prefers red to blue, or I might have been shipped off to the navy when I was ten."

It was a jest, of course. The countess doted on her sons as well as Darcy and Georgiana. She had even attempted to convince Anne to come and stay, but Lady Catherine would not relinquish her. "Do you really think she will be able to accept Miss Elizabeth, if I am able to persuade her to marry me?"

Fitzwilliam leaned forward. "Darcy, she would not accept just any woman from the country, that much is true. Not without fortune or family. But from what I have seen, as well as your description of her, Miss Elizabeth is precisely the sort of unique young woman the countess likes. If you are truly set on her, my mother will introduce her to society, put her on display, and take the credit for all of Miss Elizabeth's inevitable success. Does Miss Elizabeth play the harp?"

"Pianoforte."

"Too bad. Less fashionable. Mother may try to press her into learning, but I believe your lady can hold her own."

"I do not wish her to be required to hold her own, Fitzwilliam. I have brought her enough trouble already."

"What, Lady Catherine? I suppose you did not notice that Miss Elizabeth arrived at her uncle's home at a respectable hour, not at midnight. She seems to have withstood the old woman's demands quite handily."

"Miss Elizabeth was both harangued and denied her visit. It is a wonder Mr. Gardiner did not show us the door straight off."

"Her ability to stand against Lady Catherine's outrageous demands is something Mother will approve of. You need a wife who will be able to withstand all the cats when she is alone in their presence, Darcy, for you cannot always be with her. You are about to wave your preference for Miss Elizabeth like a flag in front of the bulls of the ton. You had better hope the girl is a *matadora*."

Darcy's smile grew slowly. "Trust me, Fitzwilliam, Miss Elizabeth is up to the task."

Lady Matlock was everything Lady Catherine was not. Compassionate, intelligent, shrewd. She did not invent gossip, but she was always keenly aware of it, using it as a form of currency that informed her social manoeuvres as well as her husband's political career. While other women of her status detested the "eccentrics" among them, Lady Matlock collected them. Her salons were legend among the best thinkers, writers, and artists of the day.

"I have invited Mrs. Franke to take tea with me," Lady Matlock said with a beneficent smile. "I presume you have something important to ask of her?"

"We do, mother," Fitzwilliam said. They waited for the countess to sit before doing so themselves.

"Your friend has been keeping company with George Wickham," Darcy informed his aunt. "We have business with him."

"I knew she had taken herself a lover, but we have not spoken since my last gathering," Lady Matlock said. "George Wickham, my goodness. I have not seen him since you boys went to Cambridge. Mrs. Franke does like a pretty face and an empty head."

"Is she aware he has hopes to marry for money?" Darcy asked. "And that he can run through a fortune faster than anyone in England?"

"Except the prince," Fitzwilliam muttered.

"Oh, do not be concerned about that," Lady Matlock replied. "She has assured me she will never remarry, and why should she? She has the respectability and the freedom she desires. Her brother is her trustee, but in name only. It is the very best of situations for her. A new husband would spoil everything."

"Good," Fitzwilliam said. "For we would like to ask for her help."

Lady Matlock pursed her lips and leaned back in her chair. "I believe I would prefer to speak with Mrs. Franke alone. She did not have a happy marriage, and it may please her to thwart you at every turn just for the satisfaction. She will speak more candidly with me, and I may have more influence with her."

"We need to know where Wickham is, Mother," Fitzwilliam said, already standing and straightening his waistcoat. "He is the reason Darcy nearly fell down the stairs at the theatre."

Darcy's aunt surveyed him. "Is that so?"

He nodded. "He shoved me as he passed. I do not know why, but I would like to ask."

Lady Matlock nodded. "Very well. And I suppose we shall have to do something about the gossip of your near fall?"

She meant Miss Elizabeth, of course. "Yes. But I am not averse to wedding Miss Elizabeth Bennet, Aunt."

Lady Matlock's delicate brows rose. "Indeed? Then why did you allow us to bundle you off to Kent?"

"I should not have," Darcy said. "As it happens, we met Miss Elizabeth upon the road. She was leaving town, too."

"Hmm."

"During my interaction with her, I have come to realise that while I *could* live my life without being married to Miss Elizabeth, I do not want to."

His aunt nodded silently. "I shall think on this," she said. "But for now, you must go."

Fitzwilliam filched a biscuit from the tea tray as it was brought in. "We shall wait in the library. You will wish to speak to me after your visit," he told her coyly. "For I have seen the wall covering you love so much in another house."

"The damask?" Aunt Matlock was alarmed.

"The very one. Please let us know if we can be of any further assistance, Mother."

Fitzwilliam's mother frowned at him. "I doubt I shall require it, dear, but if I am wrong, I shall inform you."

The men walked down the hall to the far end of the house and entered the library. Fitzwilliam sat in one of the chairs near a window, but Darcy remained standing, staring out into the small garden below.

"You are not *averse* to wedding Miss Elizabeth, eh?" Fitzwilliam asked mockingly.

"I know I am a fool, Fitzwilliam, you need not tell me." Darcy clasped his hands behind his back.

"Where is the fun in that?" Fitzwilliam crossed his legs. "You have a sort of luck I cannot fathom, Darcy. Even when you are caught in a compromising position with a young lady, she turns out to be a jewel. You need not fret about marrying her."

Darcy rocked up on his toes and back on his heels. "Ever since you and I spoke of my behaviour in Hertfordshire, I have been turning it over in my mind. She did not want an offer out of obligation."

"No good woman would."

"And this is why I am a fool, Cousin, for I love Miss Elizabeth. And yet it is only now, when I told my aunt that I was not *averse* to the marriage, that I fully understood myself. Wedding Miss Elizabeth Bennet is not something I must do to assuage my honour. It is in fact my deepest desire."

Fitzwilliam stood and put a hand on Darcy's shoulder. "Go home, Cousin. I will wait for my mother. You need to think about how you will woo your Miss Elizabeth so that she knows you have finally removed your head from your . . ."

"Enough," Darcy said.

The garden outside the window was alive with tiny green shoots that held great promise for the spring. It felt rather like a sign. "Miss Elizabeth enjoys walking. Perhaps we should start there."

Fitzwilliam chuckled. "Go home and lay your plans, Darcy. I fear you do not have a great deal of time."

"I will. And Fitzwilliam—thank you. For everything."

That night, Darcy received a note from his aunt. It stated that Mrs. Franke would bring Mr. Wickham when requested, and that Lady Matlock would let him know when that was to be.

On the third day after Elizabeth's abrupt return to Gracechurch Street, she was well enough recovered to dress and walk downstairs without any assistance.

"Good morning, Lizzy," her uncle greeted her cheerfully. "I am pleased to see you on your own two feet."

Elizabeth laughed. "Have you been waiting long to say that to me, Uncle?"

"Almost three days," Aunt Gardiner replied with a mischievous glance at her husband.

"You reveal all my secrets, Mrs. Gardiner," he said, feigning displeasure. His wife smiled at him, and he offered one of his own in return. He held up a note that had been sitting by his plate. "But here is one even you do not know. Mr. Darcy has been to see me twice at my offices, once with his cousin and once by himself. Today," he said as Jane entered the breakfast room, "Mr. Darcy will call here with Mr. Bingley. If you are all willing, and so long as Elizabeth's ankle no longer pains her, his aunt, Lady Matlock, has invited us all to a concert on Friday."

Jane's cheeks coloured, but she could not hide that she was pleased. "Thank you, Uncle Gardiner. I shall be ready to receive Mr. Bingley."

"And you, Elizabeth?" Aunt Gardiner asked. "Will you be ready to meet Mr. Darcy?"

She had spent a good deal of time in her chamber, pretending to read while she wooed herself on Mr. Darcy's behalf. Never had she felt like such a goose. He had taken the responsibility for their misunderstandings, but it had been her fault as much as his—the man's insults at the start of their acquaintance had coloured her perception of him. She had allowed her vanity to be played upon as a result. Well, she would think on that no longer.

Aunt Gardiner took her musing for indecision. "Elizabeth, consider this. Your Mr. Darcy is a powerful man and used, I would think, to having his own way."

"That is because he does not yet have a wife," Mr. Gardiner said laughingly.

"Hush, you," her aunt said affectionately.

"Yes, dear." Her uncle's eyes twinkled with delight.

"As I was saying," Aunt Gardiner continued, "he need not offer for you at all. Being willing to wait even a few days given the circumstances—that demonstrates a respect for your wishes that is very pleasing. A man who was resentful would not care about earning your good opinion."

Elizabeth nodded slowly. She quite agreed. "Then I suppose I will accept his call and his invitation for the concert."

"There now," Uncle Gardiner said, reaching for the jam, "do you see why I married her?"

"Yes, well," Aunt Gardiner said pertly, "perhaps you might remember that the next time you pass Birches in Cornhill. Last time you forgot my cheesecake."

"I ought to have known better than to offer you a compliment, my dear," he said. "For it always winds up pinching my purse."

"Your purse can manage it well enough. Lizzy," her aunt said, addressing her again, "Lady Matlock has written me to confer on how best to thwart the gossip, and I waited only your approval to respond. But know this. I do think it right to allow Mr. Darcy to press his suit, but should you learn something that makes your mutual compatibility unlikely, we will find another way to protect you."

Her uncle grunted. "Apparently the women have this well in hand."

Elizabeth felt a great rush of love for her aunt and uncle. "I thank you."

"I must thank the two of you," Aunt Gardiner said cheerfully as Uncle Gardiner served her eggs. "You and Jane are providing me with experience I shall use when my own girls begin to receive callers."

"Bite your tongue, woman," Uncle Gardiner growled. "I am on the verge of giving these two away. *My* daughters will remain at home."

Aunt Gardiner laughed. "Very well, Edward. But when the time comes, you will be announcing that news to the girls, not I. And Lizzy . . ."

"Yes?"

"Lady Matlock would like to meet you."

Elizabeth took special care with her appearance in preparation for Mr. Darcy's call. He had spent a good deal of time with Uncle Gardiner while he waited for her to be well, and that deserved some demonstration of her appreciation, did it not? Fortunately, Jane was too caught up with her own toilette to tease her sister overmuch.

"How do I look?" Jane asked anxiously.

"Stand and turn," Elizabeth said. It was a routine that calmed Jane, for though she never looked anything but perfect, she relied upon Elizabeth's approval in matters of dress.

Soon, Elizabeth thought with a little jolt to her heart, Mr. Bingley might be the one upon whom Jane relied. "You look beautiful, Jane. Mr. Bingley will be too struck to speak."

"Now you," Jane commanded, and Elizabeth stood for inspection. "Turn." She smiled. "You are so lovely, Lizzy. Perhaps Mr. Darcy will be so struck that he *does* speak."

Elizabeth cast her eyes up to the ceiling. If Mr. Bingley made Jane an offer, it should be enough to calm any gossip about Elizabeth and Mr. Darcy, and it would not matter whether he spoke or not.

"Shall I go down first, Jane?" If her sister needed a bit more time, Elizabeth would be happy to lead the way.

But Jane shook her head. "No. Together."

They arrived at the top of the stairs just as Mr. Darcy and Mr. Bingley were handing their hats to the butler. Mr. Darcy glanced up first.

Mr. Bingley might have looked up, too, but Elizabeth would not have known. For now, rested and healed, she was caught by the pleasure she saw reflected in Mr. Darcy's expressive eyes. Had she ever thought him unfeeling? How blind she had been! It was all there if one cared to look for it.

"Good day, gentlemen," she heard herself say as she and Jane glided down the steps. "Shall we go into the drawing room?"

When they arrived, Mr. Darcy drew Elizabeth to the far corner of the room, near a large window that looked out over the small garden in back. "Forgive me, Miss Elizabeth, but Bingley will need a little privacy for what he wishes to say. Your aunt said she would give him a few minutes."

"He does not plan to propose, I hope?" Jane was not ready for that. Mr. Bingley would ruin his chances if . . .

"No, but he will leave her in no doubt of his intentions."

"Good," Elizabeth said happily. "That is good."

"Now," Mr. Darcy said quietly, his gaze slipping to the side of her face where she had been bruised. Fortunately, the mark was nearly imperceptible now. "May I ask after your health?"

"I am very well, sir."

"That relieves my mind a good deal," he told her. "I cannot tell you how I felt when I thought I might have hurt you."

"You *are* rather large, but you did not injure me." Mr. Darcy pressed his lips together, but why, she could not fathom. "Said I something amiss?"

He slowly shook his head.

"Well, then, I will tell you that I was sore but not truly injured."

"I am pleased to hear it," he said hurriedly, and changed the subject. "Has Mr. Gardiner told you of my invitation?"

"Yes, he mentioned a concert."

"A small but intriguing affair, for my aunt has persuaded Mr. Clementi to conduct."

"But he has retired from performing," Elizabeth said, surprised.

"He is happier composing and publishing music these days, but my aunt suggested a fundraiser for a musical society he is attempting to organize."

"He is not a young man anymore. I cannot fault him." Elizabeth paused. "This is truly quite an extraordinary event, Mr. Darcy. How long has your aunt been planning it?"

He lifted his shoulders. "Knowing Lady Matlock? A few days." He smiled gently. "I suspect she will be filling the hall with those who are inclined to support us."

"Will your sister join us?"

"Not this time. Lady Matlock has tremendous influence, but neither she nor I wish to expose my sister to the possibility of impertinent gossip. Instead, she has arranged for Mr. Clementi to offer Georgiana a private lesson."

"Miss Darcy must be in raptures."

Mr. Darcy chuckled. "You are not wrong."

"So," Elizabeth said, taking a deep breath, "you are aware, of course, that Lady Matlock wishes to meet me."

Mr. Darcy inclined his head. "I am. She is quite anxious to make your acquaintance."

"Indeed?"

She must have appeared disconcerted, for Mr. Darcy glanced across the room to judge their privacy. Elizabeth's gaze followed. Her sister and Mr. Bingley were still sitting side by side on the settee, having a serious discussion. Mr. Darcy took her hand.

"Miss Elizabeth," he said, "I have met your family. Do you not think it fair that you should now meet mine?"

"I have already met a few members of your family, Mr. Darcy," she reminded him archly. "Thus I am uncertain how to prepare. Shall I wear a gown or a suit of armour?"

Mr. Darcy lifted her hand to his lips and bestowed a kiss upon it before releasing it. Elizabeth could hardly breathe.

"I recommend a gown, Miss Elizabeth. A very pretty gown." His lips curled into a little smile.

Despite her newly accepted feelings for the gentleman, Elizabeth did not understand how he could discompose her so thoroughly with two short sentences and a fleeting smile, nor why she wanted to be the one who made that smile appear.

"Pity about the armour," she said, "for it does fit me rather well. But if you prefer a gown, then a gown it shall be. I happen to have a few with me."

There it was again, that wavering, unsteady movement about his mouth that she knew now was an unerring sign of his amusement. She felt triumphant. She felt . . . hopeful.

Chapter Fifteen

On the following day, a week after the incident at the theatre and the second day Mr. Darcy came to call, they took his carriage to a park a few miles away.

As they strolled, Elizabeth glanced up at Mr. Darcy. Jane and Mr. Bingley were behind them, and a few steps behind them, her aunt and Vaz followed.

Elizabeth remained hopeful about Mr. Darcy's suit, but there was still something she needed to ask, and there would never be a better time. "Mr. Darcy," she said quietly, "if there was not threat of scandal, would you even have thought of me?"

He was silent for a time. The longer they strolled without speaking, the more embarrassed Elizabeth became. But she was determined to hear his answer, and at last it came.

"Forgive me for not responding immediately," he said. "I wished to think your question through, for I believe you are asking more than the question itself implies. The simple answer is I cannot say, but I believe I would. Our planned visits to Kent would have overlapped, and I am certain I could not have resisted courting you there."

"Under the nose of Lady Catherine? You are a brave man, Mr. Darcy."

"Perhaps I would have asked to call on you in London," he conceded.

Elizabeth looked straight ahead. "I realise this is abrupt, but I must say it. It is very important to me that if we wed, the marriage not be an unequal one."

Mr. Darcy grunted. "I cannot deny I might once have believed myself above you, Miss Elizabeth, but I assure you, that is no longer the case. I am now persuaded that I have much to do to deserve you."

"I do not wish you to change for me, Mr. Darcy."

"You misunderstand, Miss Elizabeth. I do not intend to change for you, but for me. Regardless of whether you can ever accept me, I wish to be the sort of man a woman of worth—a woman *like* you—would be proud to have as her husband."

She smiled weakly. "My parents, Mr. Darcy, were very much in love when they married. I have heard the stories. But when faced with the vicissitudes of life, that love diminished until it was difficult even to see. How can I know that your feelings will not wither over time?"

"Your parents' love," Mr. Darcy said slowly. "Was it built on a solid foundation?"

Elizabeth knew what he was asking. "My father was handsome and rich; my mother was beautiful and lively. They do not have much in common besides their children. And there was no heir, which I think was difficult for them both. He ignores my mother, and she goes to ever greater lengths to gain some small part of his attention. So I must say no, they wed without a proper understanding of one another. It is not the life I wish for myself."

"Very well. Let me say that you and I would begin with a different situation. We are similar in many ways, I think. We are both of a serious nature, though fortunately you possess enough good humour for the both of us. We are both protective of our families. We are both readers," he teased.

She shook her head at him but smiled.

"We enjoy Shakespeare but not the sonnets."

Her smile widened.

"We enjoy a good debate. You are even willing to profess opinions not your own for the sake of the argument. I do the same, for the mind requires exercise as much as the body." Mr. Darcy held out his arm for her, and she took it without thought.

"Pemberley is not entailed. We might leave it to a daughter or even another family member should we remain childless. But I would prefer to have children."

"As would I."

"Although I believe I could produce more examples of ways in which we are compatible, let me only add this. A clever wife is essential to me, for Pemberley is a lifelong responsibility, and needs many good minds to help tend it."

"You would take my advice about your estate?"

"If it is good advice," he teased, and then studied her for a moment. "When you said that you wished for admiration and respect, this is what you meant? That you do not see either between your parents?"

Elizabeth closed her eyes. "It is painful to speak of it, but yes."

"Open your eyes, Miss Elizabeth," he told her kindly. "Look at me."

She did.

"You have no reason to be distressed. Every wife should want those things from her husband. Every wife should expect them. And if we do conclude this business of ours with a marriage, I will make you a promise. We may disagree or even argue, but you will always have my respect, and I do not expect that my admiration for you will ever fade." He patted her hand as it lay on his arm.

"It is an odd sort of courtship we are enjoying," Elizabeth said wistfully. "Is it strange to feel I know more about you than if our acquaintance had been filled with visits in drawing rooms and brief walks about the garden?"

"Not at all," Mr. Darcy replied. "I believe that in the crisis of the past days, we have each revealed more of our true natures than is typically done. I have been very pleased with what I have learned of you."

"And I of you."

His chest swelled, and she glanced away. "Do not burst your buttons, Mr. Darcy. There is work yet to do."

He dipped his head and spoke gently in her ear. "Not for you."

By the time he straightened, Aunt Gardiner was approaching. It was time to return to the house. Elizabeth had a great deal to think about, not the least of which was Mr. Darcy's promise.

That evening, Elizabeth donned a gown her aunt and uncle had gifted her and attempted not to wrinkle it as she sat in the carriage that would carry her to tea with Lady Matlock. The invitation was for Elizabeth and Mrs. Gardiner only. Mr. Darcy had confided that his aunt had directed the men in the family not to intrude.

"Aunt Gardiner, I do not understand how you can remain so calm!" she exclaimed.

"It is quite simple, Elizabeth," her aunt replied. "I am calm because I am not the one being evaluated this evening."

Elizabeth squirmed on the bench. Fortunately, there were fewer carriages on the road just now, and they arrived at Matlock House in relatively short order.

A tall, heavy butler with a dour expression showed them in. He escorted them to a small parlour, where a maid was just setting down a tea tray.

Mrs. Gardiner and Miss Elizabeth Bennet to see you, my lady."

Lady Matlock dismissed her servants, and the three of them were left alone. Elizabeth tried not to fidget as the countess examined them. "Good evening, ladies."

They curtsied.

The countess was taller than Lady Catherine had been, and younger. Her hair was styled elaborately, and her gown was fashionable and expensive. Most disconcerting, however, was her gaze, which was both shrewd and exacting.

Elizabeth felt her hands twitch.

"I understand this is irregular, Miss Elizabeth," Lady Matlock said, "but would you be so kind as to pour?"

It *was* irregular, but despite the fire and many lit candles, the room was a little dark. Perhaps it was difficult for Lady Matlock to see.

"Certainly," Elizabeth replied, and moved to do so.

The ritual calmed her, and when everyone had been served, she sat down next to Aunt Gardiner with her tea and a good deal more confidence.

"Now, Miss Elizabeth," the countess said, lifting her cup, "I am told you wish to wed my nephew."

Elizabeth felt her aunt stiffen, but she did not speak. "That is not entirely accurate, Lady Matlock."

"No?"

There were a hundred meanings in that single word, but Elizabeth would not play such games.

"No, my lady."

"He is very wealthy."

"Forgive me, Lady Matlock, but there are more important things in a marriage than wealth."

"I should like to know what they are," the countess replied, clearly amused at Elizabeth's naiveté.

"A sufficient income is necessary, of course," Elizabeth said thoughtfully. "But Mr. Darcy's wealth far exceeds what I would require. It is of more importance to me that there be mutual regard and respect."

"And this you do not expect from my nephew?"

Elizabeth exchanged a glance with her aunt. "He is making his case, Lady Matlock."

"Indeed?" the august lady inquired. "And are you making yours?"

Aunt Gardiner cleared her throat very softly in warning, but Elizabeth felt it necessary to tell the countess everything. "The case I have made is only to request Mr. Darcy defer a proposal for a time. I have hopes that another scandal might divert the attentions of those who would denigrate us. After all, there are scandalous stories printed in the newspapers every week. My mother is quite devoted to them."

The countess laughed aloud and then fixed her gaze upon Elizabeth. "How very astute. Such tales *are* often replaced by something even more . . . unexpected."

The lady then turned her attention to Aunt Gardiner and nimbly extracted a great deal of information about Uncle Gardiner's business. Not that Elizabeth's aunt was loath to give it, for she was very proud of her husband.

"Mrs. Gardiner," Lady Matlock said after a half an hour had passed, "would you remain behind for a moment?"

Elizabeth understood that this was a dismissal. She rose, set her teacup on a silver tray, and politely took her leave.

"What did Lady Matlock have to say?" she inquired once they were on their way back to Gracechurch Street.

"She wished to tell me how much she likes you," Aunt Gardiner replied. "And to ask me about my wallpaper."

On Thursday, Darcy and Bingley stayed to dinner at Gracechurch Street. Friday, they all visited Gunter's, including Fitzwilliam, though the weather was still rather grey, and they ordered tea rather than ices. Miss Elizabeth begged rather prettily to extend that trip to Hatchards, which had earned her Darcy's quick agreement. If he ever needed to apologise to her when they were married—*if* they married, he scolded himself—he need not pluck all the flowers in the garden. He could instead take her to look at books, something that would give him pleasure as well.

Despite these outings, thus far no one had accosted them, and Darcy was relieved. Being seen in a large family party had been an excellent notion after all.

He had hoped but not really expected it to last. When the first blow came, however, it was not from anyone who had been in the theatre that night. It was from another source altogether.

"Brother!" Miss Bingley called on the morning of the concert. There was another woman with her, tall and elegantly formed. "Whatever do you do here?"

They were all strolling through Hyde Park. It was just after breakfast and long before the fashionable hour, for while Miss Elizabeth adored the park, she had told Darcy that she had no desire to give rise to further gossip. He fell back to walk with her uncle when he saw who was approaching. Mrs. Gardiner stepped up to take his place with Miss Elizabeth.

"Good morning, Caroline, Miss Grantley," Mr. Bingley replied easily. "We are walking, as you see."

Miss Bingley's smile dripped with condescension.

"We hardly see you now that you are staying with Mr. Darcy, Charles," she said, no doubt for Miss Grantley's benefit. Then she turned her eye to Bingley's companion. "My goodness, Miss Bennet, here you are. I thought you had returned to Hertfordshire long ago," Miss Bingley said smoothly. "And Miss Elizabeth, of course. Where one sister is to be found, so shall the other. Mr. Darcy," she added, dropping into a curtsy for him alone. "Good day to you, sir."

Mr. Bingley's smile was every bit as hard as his sister's. "Have you a faulty memory, sister? For you were introduced to Mrs. Gardiner when you called upon Miss Bennet in Gracechurch Street this winter."

Miss Bingley flinched but did not falter. Her eyes shot to Darcy's, but he only gazed steadily back at her. Miss Elizabeth turned to look at him and then back to Miss Bingley.

Bingley did not miss the exchange either, for he held out his arm to indicate their other guest. "Mr. Gardiner, may I present my sister Miss Caroline Bingley?"

Uncle Gardiner touched the brim of his hat. "Miss Bingley."

Miss Grantley glanced at Miss Bingley and raised her eyebrows. If Miss Bingley was surprised that her amiable brother would both call her out publicly *and* offer Mr. Gardiner precedence in the introductions, she did not show it.

"It *is* a shame you have not responded to my notes," Mr. Bingley replied. "For we shall all be attending the Clementi concert tonight. Had you replied sooner, you might have secured an invitation. Perhaps they both went astray?"

Miss Bingley's complexion paled.

"Oh, the Clementi concert," Miss Grantley exclaimed. "How delightful!" She smiled cloyingly at Mr. Bingley. "Surely you might have room for a few more."

"I am afraid not, Miss Grantley," Darcy said, moving closer to Miss Elizabeth. The note of satisfaction in his tone was so complete that Miss Elizabeth pressed her lips together to keep from laughing. "It is a private concert and my aunt has now extended all her invitations."

"Of course," Miss Grantley replied, shooting a dissatisfied look at Miss Bingley. "Do enjoy yourself."

"I believe we shall," Darcy said. He offered his arm to Miss Elizabeth, and she took it. Miss Bingley's eyes widened in panic as her eyes darted between them. "Good day, ladies." He stepped off, nearly dragging Elizabeth with him.

"Sir, your legs are rather long," she hissed at him.

"I do beg your pardon," Darcy said, slowing his pace.

"Thank you," she said, and bit her lips.

"What?"

A small laugh burst from her. "The silent conversation you and Miss Bingley were having was quite amusing. She was in a sinking boat, and you refused to bail her out."

"Of course you saw that," he grumbled. "You miss nothing."

"You may not have used words, but your meaning was clear."

"Miss Elizabeth," he said, rubbing a hand over his face, "you read me very well."

"It is not difficult now that I know what to look for. I thought you very like her, once."

Darcy groaned. "Do not say so."

"But it is true," she said earnestly. "I *did* think that. Now that you have told me what was weighing on you last autumn, I think perhaps you *wanted* to be like Miss Bingley. Your feelings were painful to you, and you wished to inure yourself to them."

Miss Elizabeth was so perceptive. "I had not thought of that, but I think you must be right."

"I do not mean to offend, Mr. Darcy. It is easier to see these things in others than in oneself, that is all." She offered him a sheepish smile.

"You do not give yourself enough credit, Miss Elizabeth."

"Oh," she warned him with a glint in her eye, "that is not a fault of mine."

"Lizzy," Jane said as she approached, "Uncle and Aunt Gardiner wish to return home now. Are you ready?"

"Of course," Miss Elizabeth replied. "Mr. Darcy, will you and Mr. Bingley join us for refreshments?"

Miss Bennet's smile was serene, but she nearly glowed with happiness. Darcy cursed himself as a fool. How could he not have seen how different her smiles were for his friend?

"I believe I can answer for Bingley," he said. "We should be delighted."

An hour later, Aunt Gardiner was ordering tea and cakes and brought the children down to the drawing room for a visit. For some reason, they had bobbed hasty greetings to Mr. Bingley but then gathered around Mr. Darcy.

Mr. Darcy, who now stood straight and tall, was closely inspecting the four small Gardiners before him.

"Very well," he said. "I believe I have it now." He bowed to the eldest girl. "Miss Emily, ten years of age."

Emily nodded demurely and curtsied.

Mr. Darcy moved to the next child. "And this is Miss Arabella, but you prefer Miss Bella, eight years of age."

Bella lifted herself on her toes and then dropped rather dramatically into a wobbly curtsy. Mr. Darcy stifled a smile and offered her a bow.

"This," he said sternly, moving down the line, "is Master Harry, five years of age."

"He is right, Emmie!" the boy cried. "He 'member'd!"

"Bow, Harry," Bella said, poking him.

Harry did. Mr. Darcy reciprocated, and then stopped to stare at the youngest, appearing to think it over. "Hm. Difficult," he said, and the children loudly encouraged him. "No, no, do not tell me." He held up a hand, then walked all the way around the youngest Gardiner, nodding to himself.

Elizabeth caught Jane's eye, and they both stifled a laugh. Who knew Mr. Darcy could be so playful?

Mr. Bingley shook his head. "Darcy loves children," he told them quietly. "He was his sister's guardian, you know."

"I have it!" Mr. Darcy exclaimed. "This is Master Nicholas, who is three."

"Al'mos' four!" Nicholas protested.

"Ah, but almost four is still three. You must not be in such a hurry to grow up, Master Nicholas." Mr. Darcy crouched down until they were nearly eye-to-eye. "There is plenty of time for that."

Nicholas threw his arms around Mr. Darcy's neck. The man was startled, but recovered quickly, placing one large hand on the boy's back and patting it awkwardly.

"He knows all our names, Lizzy," Emily said, sitting on the settee and curling up between her two cousins. "No one ever remembers us all, not properly."

"Emily, posture," her mother said from where she had just pulled the bell. Emily uncurled her legs and sat up.

"Would you like to help me serve?" Aunt Gardiner asked her eldest.

"Oh, may I?" Emily cried. "I mean, yes, please, Mamma."

As Aunt Gardiner directed Emily on how best to pour her guests' tea, Mr. Darcy sat down on a chair across the room and began to comment on the various toy soldiers that were thrust in his direction. "This is a grenadier," he told them. "We no longer have grenadiers in the army. They have become the Life Guards now."

"How he keeps it all straight is beyond me," Mr. Bingley said with an admiring grin. "I suppose his cousin Colonel Fitzwilliam has tutored him."

"Will we see the colonel at the concert?" Jane asked.

"I doubt his mother would appreciate him missing it," Mr. Bingley replied.

Jane agreed that it must be so, and as so often occurred, she and Mr. Bingley were soon in a conversation that left Elizabeth without any need to participate. She watched Mr. Darcy carefully as he patiently inspected every toy the boys dragged over to him.

"I like Mr. Darcy, Lizzy," Bella confided as Nicholas offered him a tiny bugle and Mr. Darcy pretended he could not make it work.

Elizabeth dropped a kiss on the top of Bella's head and, though her cousin really was too old, allowed Bella to climb up on her lap and hand her a book. "I do too," she replied.

Bella leaned her head against Elizabeth's shoulder while Elizabeth read to her.

After a time, the boys ran out of toys to show Mr. Darcy and they were drawn to the story, dropping on the rug at Elizabeth's feet. She smiled at them and looked up to see how Mr. Darcy fared.

He was watching her as he often did, dark eyes blazing with something that made her blush. It was all she could do to finish the book before their tea and cakes arrived. A good thing, too, for new friends and stories were nothing to cake. As she was abandoned by her cousins, Mr. Darcy handed her a teacup.

"Miss Emily is handling the pouring very well," he said.

"My aunt is an excellent teacher," Elizabeth said.

"They are rather remarkable children," Mr. Darcy said his own teacup suspended in the air. "Very well behaved."

"Is that what you call it?" Elizabeth was vastly amused. "The boys dragged out every item they owned for your approval."

"And some that they did not," Mr. Darcy informed her with a chuckle. "They also put them all away when their mother directed them. Yes, I called them well behaved, and I meant it."

"You are very good with them."

"Children have no artifice," Mr. Darcy said, taking another cup of tea from Emily and thanking her. "It is easier to understand them."

Every hour she spent with Mr. Darcy, Elizabeth thought as she took a sip of her tea, made it easier to understand him, too.

Chapter Sixteen

Darcy's mouth was as dry as sand. When he had teased Miss Elizabeth about her gown earlier in the week, he had forgotten that her uncle was a purveyor of fine silks. A deadly miscalculation, for now he could barely speak, and the words that he had managed to form made no sense, at least, not to him.

It wasn't the fashionable jonquil colour of her dress, though it suited her, or the expensive silken lace trimming the short sleeves and hem that held his attention. It was the cut of the gown, how it skimmed Miss Elizabeth's light and pleasing figure, suggesting without revealing. It was the enticing embroidery of the bodice that drew attention to—well, the display was modest by the standards of the ton, but more daring than anything he had yet seen Miss Elizabeth wear. That was what was causing his heart to race, for it was certainly not the memory of their fall and where, precisely, he had landed.

Not even at Bingley's ball had Miss Elizabeth been so richly attired. Miss Bennet wore a gown similarly fitted—Bingley would be captivated—but Darcy could not spend any time thinking of Miss Bennet when Miss Elizabeth was so near.

Once they had sat in near silence for the first five minutes, Darcy managed to breathe deeply and say, "Your gowns are very fine, ladies."

Mr. Gardiner chuckled from his position next to Darcy. "They ought to be. My lovely bride has her choice of the silks as they are finished, and she has an excellent eye."

Mrs. Gardiner smiled at her husband.

"We keep our best gowns here in town, Mr. Darcy," Miss Elizabeth told him, and he detected some smugness on her part. "Parties in Hertfordshire rarely require such finery."

Darcy nodded. "That is wise." What was he saying? Utter nonsense. He glanced at her, trying to regain his bearings.

Whatever it was that he had said or done, Miss Elizabeth was nearly beaming at him, and he was determined to keep her as pleased with him as she seemed to be now.

"We thought an introduction to your family important enough for our best," Miss Bennet added.

At last, something he could hang a conversation on. "Indeed. I have heard Clementi perform before, but it has been several years."

"And what shall we hear tonight?" Mrs. Gardiner asked.

"I believe Schobert, Beethoven, and perhaps a bit of Clementi's own work, but of course, he may change his mind before the performance."

"That sounds wonderful," Miss Elizabeth said enthusiastically. "I have always admired his Sonata in B flat major, which I believe Herr Mozart studied extensively for his opera."

"My sister mentioned something similar, Miss Elizabeth," he replied. "She showed me his score, in which he specifically notes that the composition date is earlier than *The Magic Flute*."

"It is too bad he must defend his own work," Mr. Gardiner declared. "But it is often the way of the world. Those who come before pave the way, but rarely do they receive the credit for it."

Everyone made their way out to the carriage, but Darcy had misplaced one of his warm gloves. Miss Elizabeth tarried to help him locate it. When the hall was clear, he reached into his coat pocket and rolled his eyes. "Never mind." He held it up, and Miss Elizabeth laughed as he slid it on.

Her eyes sparkled in the candlelight. That dress, that smile, those eyes—his chest tightened, and his breath caught.

Do not risk it, he warned himself. *It is too soon.*

"Miss Elizabeth," he said softly, "I wish to ask you a question."

"Yes, Mr. Darcy?" she inquired, glancing towards the door.

Thank goodness for his gloves; perhaps Miss Elizabeth would not feel how damp they were as he took her hands. "Before we enter the fray this evening, I would like to know whether your mind has been changed at all. About me, that is. Whether you would consent to . . ."

Her eyes were watching him carefully, alight with laughter.

"I am not making any sense," he said, chagrined.

"You are making perfect sense, Mr. Darcy."

"Elizabeth! Darcy! We are awaiting you!" Uncle Gardiner cried from outside.

Mr. Darcy still held her hands. Elizabeth stood on her tiptoes, and he leaned down so she could whisper something in his ear.

He was not a man whose happiness overflowed in mirth, but the smile he bestowed upon her sent a frisson of heat all the way down to her toes.

"Here now, what are you two about?" Uncle Gardiner asked from just outside the open front door.

"Nothing, sir," Elizabeth called.

Mr. Darcy offered her his arm as Uncle Gardiner disappeared into the dark again. "Everything," he told Elizabeth, shaking his head a little as if in disbelief. "Everything."

Miss Elizabeth's face was glowing with excitement as they approached the Argyll Rooms, where the concert was to be held. When the carriage arrived at the entrance, he nearly leapt out of the carriage before the steps had been set, for he could not remain in close quarters with her while she looked so enchanting.

Mr. Gardiner exited next, then assisted his wife and Miss Bennet, offering each of them an arm once they stood beside him.

Miss Elizabeth's smile had his heart pounding. She slid her delicate hand into his larger one and stepped down with the ease and elegance that he adored.

"Thank you, Mr. Darcy," she said warmly as he offered her his arm. "Do not fear, we all know our parts." Hers was to be the charming young woman with pert opinions the countess appeared to favour. His was to be the besotted lover.

He was no actor, but this would be a simple role for him to play. "Are you ready to defeat the ton?" he inquired.

"My goodness," Miss Elizabeth replied. "Perhaps I ought to have chosen the armour after all." She placed her hand in the crook of his elbow.

Darcy glanced down and their eyes met. His heart thrilled, for never had she gazed at him so tenderly.

"No need," he said hoarsely. "For you are with me."

When they entered the lobby, Bingley was already there, Miss Bennet on his arm. Next to them stood the Gardiners, appearing handsome, prosperous, and fashionable.

"Darcy!" exclaimed a familiar voice. Heads turned at his entrance. "Well met!"

Fitzwilliam strode across the hall, resplendent in his red coat, medals and ribbons pinned across his chest. He spoke the name of each member of the party clearly as he greeted them. How different from just over a week ago, when Darcy had dared not speak Miss Elizabeth's name at the theatre!

The hall where they would hear the concert held only thirty people, and the tiny lobby was beginning to fill. Fitzwilliam made his way inside, stopping to speak with several other men.

"Oh, no," he protested rather loudly. "I was the one who ran into Darcy. Do not know my own strength!" He laughed, and someone clapped him on the arm.

Darcy leaned over to Elizabeth. "That is the Viscount Milton," he whispered, indicating a dandy who was headed their way. "Fitzwilliam's elder brother. They are alike only in essentials."

As though he had heard Darcy, though from his distance he could not possibly have done so, Milton lifted his hand in a half wave. He said something to his friend and made his way over to their group.

"This is great fun," he said with a superior waggle of his eyebrows. "We have not had to protect a member of the family in an age." His gaze took them all in but settled upon Miss Bennet. "Who are *these* lovely creatures?" he crooned.

Milton felt every bit of his elevated status, to be sure, but he was too much his father's son to be a debaucher. It was sometimes pleasing to him to be believed one, however. It kept ambitious fathers from putting their daughters forward for his consideration. When the time came that Milton sought a wife, he would choose his own.

"Could do worse, Darcy," he said in an aside, after having been introduced to everyone present. "The sister is the real beauty, but yours is still quite pretty, and they seem to have enough feathers to fly with."

Miss Elizabeth did look the part of an heiress tonight, and Darcy would not enlighten the viscount. She was still on his arm but was speaking with her sister, Bingley, and Fitzwilliam, so missed Milton's comment.

"Stop it," he hissed at his eldest cousin. "Make us look good tonight, Milton."

His cousin scoffed. "Make *you* look good, more like. A woman who has not instantly fallen for the Darcy . . . property. Perhaps I ought to know her better. With me she would have a fortune *and* a title."

Darcy's glare was colder than a Thames frost fair.

Milton chuckled. "All right, Darcy, m'boy, all right." He held up his hands. "Fair is fair, you and Bingley saw them first."

Darcy opened his mouth to say something scathing, but the Earl and Countess chose that moment to make their appearance.

His aunt really did have an impeccable sense of timing.

The crowd parted slightly to allow them through and though they nodded at their acquaintances, they made a point of greeting Mr. and Mrs. Gardiner. His aunt and Elizabeth's spoke a few words and smiled. He watched them carefully. They were up to something.

Then the earl and countess made their way to Darcy.

"Nephew!" Lord Matlock cried, quite enjoying himself if his boisterousness was anything to judge by. "This must be Miss Elizabeth, I think?"

Elizabeth curtsied and Darcy introduced them, then the others.

"Lovely to see you again, Miss Elizabeth," the countess said, and very soon led her away. Darcy was briefly jealous of his own aunt, though her public approval and intention to introduce both Miss Bennet and Miss Elizabeth to her powerful friends in attendance was the very purpose of the evening.

"You are absurd," Milton told him. "Mother is introducing her around the room, not tossing her out the window. Despite your instructions, I do wish you would try to appear more a man and less a mooncalf."

Darcy frowned.

Milton chuckled. "Better. Now, I must know where you found these delectable creatures. Are there any more sisters?"

"Yes," Darcy replied drolly. "Would you like to meet them?"

Milton narrowed his eyes. "Not if you *wish* me to. That speaks of villainy."

The soft sound of delighted laughter wafted over the crowd to their ears. Miss Elizabeth was standing next to the countess and telling a story. Suddenly several of the women were eyeing him and tittering again.

His cravat was too tight. He ran his finger under the cloth, and the tittering increased. What was she telling them?

Milton was grinning like a fool. "I think Miss Elizabeth is going to make you a far more interesting object, Darcy. I must thank her for that."

And then Milton was off, in direct contradiction to his mother's edicts, joining the ladies, drawing their attention by telling a story just this side of wicked and making them all blush while Aunt Matlock glared at him.

Darcy tried to enter into a conversation with the Gardiners, but his eyes continually strayed to Miss Elizabeth.

The Gardiners approached after Milton's abandonment so that he would not be standing alone. They spoke around him, doing a creditable job of making him appear to be participating. At last, he glanced over at Miss Elizabeth only to see her looking back at him. She smiled a little, a mischievous expression, and arched one brow. Then she returned her attention to her companions as though that one look had not set his blood afire.

The four ladies gathered around the countess were unaccountably pleased to request introductions to Elizabeth and her sister. While they were perfectly polite to Jane, they quickly ignored her.

Elizabeth might have felt the slight to her sister, but Jane appeared relieved to continue her conversation with Mr. Bingley and the colonel.

"You must tell us what you did to catch Mr. Darcy's eye, dear," said the oldest of the gathered women, a Mrs. Farthington-Spit. "Lady Matlock says the story is most entertaining."

"I have not done anything, in fact," Elizabeth replied politely. "He was rude to me, you know, and I refused to dance with him."

"Ah," said Lady Slater knowingly. "Some men want what they cannot have."

"Now, you know my nephew is not one of *that* sort," the countess said. "He is particular, that is all."

"I should say so," Elizabeth replied before thinking it through. She nearly bit her tongue, but the words were already out of her mouth.

Lady Matlock was not angry, she was encouraging. "What do you mean, Miss Elizabeth? If you have something to report about my nephew, I should dearly like to hear it."

Well, it was too late now. "Mr. Darcy," Elizabeth said mischievously, "has an extensive list of attributes he maintains before he will allow a woman to be truly accomplished."

"What is on this list, Miss Elizabeth?" Lady Ellen asked. She was younger than the other ladies, only a few years older than Elizabeth herself.

"Let me see whether I can recall it all." She tapped her own fan to her lips. "He did say that only half a dozen women of his acquaintance were truly accomplished, by his estimation." With each successive item added to Mr. Darcy's requirements, the women gasped, smirked, and tut-tutted. "And of course," Elizabeth concluded, "such a woman must always be improving her mind through extensive reading."

"My goodness," the countess said, her eyes bright with merriment. "Other than the reading, it sounds more like Miss Bingley's list than my nephew's." She turned to her friends. "From what I am told of her, of course."

"I believe Miss Bingley did have a hand in compiling it," Elizabeth admitted, "but Mr. Darcy did not correct her."

"How did you respond, Miss Elizabeth?" asked Lady Ralston.

"I said that I was surprised at his knowing only six such ladies. I rather wondered at his knowing any."

The women deployed their fans all at once and laughed heartily behind them.

"Oh, Adele," Lady Slater said slyly to Lady Matlock, "I do see why you like her."

"And why your nephew has chosen her, though she is so unknown." Lady Ralston closed her fan in one practised flip of her wrist. "She shall be a perfect addition to your salons."

"Precisely," Lady Matlock said, offering her friends a regal nod. "She is simply marvellous."

Elizabeth glanced over her shoulder and found herself the object of Mr. Darcy's molten gaze. She smiled and lifted one brow at him before turning back to the ladies.

Lady Ellen had seen that look, for she employed her fan assiduously, as though she was overheated, and then winked at Elizabeth. Winked!

Miss Farthington-Spit said nothing, but she offered Lady Matlock a slight nod.

"I would like to hear more, Miss Elizabeth," Lady Matlock said with the same smugness of Longbourn's tabby when he had caught himself a mouse. "What are your impressions of London?"

Chapter Seventeen

"There is Picton," Mr. Gardiner said to his wife.

Darcy watched as Mr. Picton strolled over. "Good evening, Gardiner, Mrs. Gardiner," he said.

"You said you would come," Mr. Gardiner admitted, "but I was anxious. Good to see you. Makes this place feel a bit less like a foreign country."

"Your wife invited me. Who was I to say no?" Mr. Picton greeted Mrs. Gardiner warmly. When they had done, Darcy asked to be introduced as well, and Mr. Gardiner quickly complied.

"Are both your nieces with you tonight?" Picton asked.

"They are," Mr. Gardiner said. "Lizzy is with the countess, and Jane is there, you see, near her, speaking with the earl, the viscount, and Mr. Bingley."

"Difficult to believe our little girls are conversing with earls and countesses." Picton's expression softened. "They have grown into lovely young women."

"Seems like yesterday they came to stay with us following the wedding," Mr. Gardiner said, the faint trace of a smile on his lips. He turned to his wife. "Lizzy was ten?"

"And quite a handful even then," Mrs. Gardiner said teasingly.

"Oh, I recall," Mr. Picton replied. "She nearly overset a giant set of shelves diving under them to catch a kitten. When she pulled him out, she was pitch-black from all the coal dust. Then Miss Jane gave her the sweetest scolding I ever heard, and little Lizzy apologised straight away. But not for nearly being flattened or even ruining her dress. She was sorry for having frightened me."

Darcy smiled to himself. Yes, that sounded right.

Mr. Picton leaned in. "What was all that in the afternoon paper, Gardiner? Were the toffs talking about our girl?" He glanced at Darcy. "I saw what happened that night, and I know Miss Elizabeth was not to blame."

Mr. Gardiner's brows pinched together. "Which paper?"

"The *Examiner*. Here." Picton reached into his jacket. "I thought I would tuck the piece away in case you had not seen it. There is only one E.B. from L in Hertfordshire I know, but I knew if they were saying it was our Miss Elizabeth who had done such things, they are all of them liars."

Darcy's heart hammered against his chest as he read the small blurb in the gossip column. Squeezed between the Duke of Albany's reputed duel and the exploits of a member of the four-in-hand club who had knocked over several merchant stalls when he overset his speeding carriage, was an entry about an FD from Derbyshire. This man, the paragraph claimed, kept a mistress in Hertfordshire, Miss EB, originally from the estate of L, who had sprained her ankle and had accosted him at the theatre.

Many witnesses heard the esteemed FD insist that the woman remove herself from his person and yet the little baggage pulled him atop her in a most lewd display.

Who would have sold such a thing to the *Examiner*? For a moment he wondered whether Miss Bingley had done so, but she had not been in the theatre that night, nor had anyone who would speak with her. And despite seeing him with Miss Elizabeth in Hyde Park, Darcy was sure Miss Bingley still held out hope to maintain the connection, even if it was not as his wife.

No, it would not have been Miss Bingley.

Wickham, though. Miss Elizabeth had seen him. Had he seen her? They had been friendly in Hertfordshire, though Darcy knew that would not have prevented Wickham from selling Miss Elizabeth's name if it brought him a single bit of extra coin.

Darcy reached out to grab Mr. Gardiner's wrist. "I spoke with my aunt earlier today, and she must already be aware. Please, Mr. Gardiner, we must allow this evening to unfold."

"As much as I dislike it, Mr. Darcy," Mr. Gardiner replied, "I agree."

"We spoke with your aunt and uncle as we made up the guest list together," Mrs. Gardiner said calmly. "Mrs. Farthington-Spit is an acquaintance of mine who writes, on occasion, for the *Sun*. A small gift of silk and the promise of an excellent story were enough to ensure her attendance."

Darcy sighed, relieved. That the earl and countess had consented to work with Mr. and Mrs. Gardiner was a surprise, but it should not have been. His aunt did enjoy flaunting her position to make friends in what might be considered unusual places. "The *Examiner*'s rival."

Mrs. Gardiner smiled. "Just so."

Mr. Gardiner added, very quietly, "It is not only Elizabeth's reputation that is at stake tonight. This will touch all her sisters and my own family as well. We were determined to be involved."

"Her reputation, and all of yours, will be safe. Between Bingley and I . . ."

Fitzwilliam was at his shoulder, then. "We will see your family right, Mr. Gardiner," he said.

Mr. Gardiner glanced at Darcy, Fitzwilliam, and Picton. "My wife has seen to that," he informed them proudly. "She and Lady Matlock are a formidable pair."

"When Jane and Elizabeth wed," Mrs. Gardiner said, her eyes on Darcy, "we shall be nigh unstoppable."

"I will stay on your good side, Mrs. Gardiner," Fitzwilliam said, and for once, he was not jesting.

Something was changing in the air around her. Elizabeth could feel the light chatter and anticipation for the evening curdling at the edges. Before she could ask Lady Matlock what was happening, Mr. Darcy was at her side, offering his arm to lead her into the performance.

"We were identified in the gossip column of a prominent paper this afternoon," he told her very quietly. "I believe everyone is making the connection now."

Elizabeth's limbs nearly failed her, and she briefly leaned on Mr. Darcy for support. An icy dread clawed its way to her heart. "We must leave immediately." Her breaths came a little quicker.

"Trust me, Miss Elizabeth," he said, placing a hand over hers. Elizabeth revelled in its warmth. "My aunt and uncle, as well as yours, have this well in hand."

Elizabeth stopped for a moment while the small crowd surged around them. She looked up at Mr. Darcy, trying to read his expression.

It felt a little like standing at the top of those stairs that had frightened her only the week before. Her stomach tumbled and she felt vaguely ill. But this time, it was Mr. Darcy holding on to her; it was he who would not let *her* fall.

"Very well, Mr. Darcy. I trust you to see me through."

Mr. Darcy's eyes never left her own as he brushed his lips against the back of her hand. "To hear you say so . . . it is my great honour, Miss Elizabeth," he told her sombrely.

They took their seats and listened to a full program of exquisite music, Elizabeth always keenly aware of Mr. Darcy's solid presence at her side.

The concert concluded. The audience applauded. And Elizabeth stood, taking Mr. Darcy's arm once again as though nothing salacious had ever been printed about them.

"Let us allow the crowd to precede us," he told her.

Elizabeth swallowed and straightened. "Very well," she said. "I am in your hands, Mr. Darcy."

He smiled down at her, in a way that was almost reverent.

Their party was quite large by this time, making up ten of the thirty assembled guests. Lord and Lady Matlock led the way, the viscount close behind. The colonel remained on Elizabeth's left side while Mr. Darcy was on her right. Mr. Bingley and Jane and Uncle and Aunt Gardiner walked just behind. Thus assembled, they began the march towards their carriages and freedom.

"Darcy!" cried a familiar voice, and Mr. Darcy stiffened.

"Wickham," he said, turning to face the man.

Wickham was well dressed, a comely woman in her late thirties on his arm.

"Mrs. Franke," Lady Matlock said, her skirts swinging as she strode over to them. "Thank you for coming."

"We were very nearly late," the woman said, tapping Lady Matlock's arm once, lightly, with her fan. "I believe we were given the wrong time."

"Oh, I do apologise," Lady Matlock said, clearly not at all upset by her error. "I presume you were still able to enjoy the music."

"It was wonderful," Mrs. Franke said, happy to allow Lady Matlock to draw her away.

"George Wickham," Colonel Fitzwilliam said from his position behind the man. My goodness, the colonel was stealthy.

"Fitzwilliam," Mr. Wickham replied with less confidence. "You would not want to create a scene here. Such a lovely evening—it would be a shame to ruin it with talk of a scandal." He grinned at Mr. Darcy and then raked Elizabeth over with his gaze.

"Oh, that is no matter," Colonel Fitzwilliam said easily. "Everyone here was invited by my mother and Mrs. Gardiner."

"It is a surprise to see *you* here, Wickham" Mr. Darcy said. "Is not your betrothed back in Meryton?"

"Of course not." Mr. Wickham waved an arm.

"She is," Elizabeth insisted, offended for the girl. "You are engaged to Miss Mary King."

Mr. Darcy pressed her hand, and Elizabeth reluctantly stopped speaking.

"Miss King aside, I would like to know why you tried to kill my cousin at the theatre last week." Colonel Fitzwilliam's tone was conversational, but there was something dangerous beneath the words.

"Kill?" Mr. Wickham rolled his eyes, something she had never seen a man do in public. "You can be so melodramatic, Fitzwilliam. I simply did not want Darcy to see me with Mrs. Franke and try to warn her away. If he had given me the living as his father had wanted . . ."

"Please, Mr. Wickham," Miss Elizabeth said sharply. "It is a wonder you do not burst into flame with as many lies as you tell."

"They do pay me a pretty penny, though," he said charmingly, unaware of someone else approaching him from the back.

"Is that your way of saying you were paid to lie to the *Examiner*?" Miss Elizabeth asked. Mr. Wickham just smiled.

"I would like to know the answer to that, Mr. Wickham," Mrs. Farthington-Spit said flatly.

Mr. Wickham turned towards her, his smile tightening a little. "I told only the absolute truth, madam," he replied handsomely. "For I was there in the theatre that night and saw it all."

"You pushed Mr. Darcy as you rushed down the stairs, I presume leaving Mrs. Franke behind," Miss Elizabeth said. "That qualifies you as a coward, not a witness."

"Mrs. Franke was a dozen feet away, speaking with her husband's family. She asked me to go downstairs and wait for her, that is all."

"I see. Her family disapproves of you."

Mr. Wickham shrugged.

Elizabeth seethed. How could she ever have thought this man charming?

Colonel Fitzwilliam cleared his throat. "So you had been dismissed by Mrs. Franke, and, like the good little boy you are, you headed for the stairs. But you realised that Darcy was there, and you did not want to chance his speaking with Mrs. Franke's family about you."

"Ending any chance of making more money from the woman," Mr. Darcy said, completing his cousin's thought.

Colonel Fitzwilliam chuckled. "I suppose that makes *you* the mistress, eh, Wickham?"

Mr. Darcy cleared his throat loudly. "*Fitz.*" He tipped his head at Elizabeth.

He was a dear man to protect her sensibilities. Too bad he had not been there to prevent Charlotte from attacking them.

"I presume, then, that you are the one who yelled 'fire'?" Elizabeth asked. "As a distraction, since Mr. Darcy was between you and the exit?"

"Of course not," Mr. Wickham said, so smoothly that he fooled no one.

"You meant to use the commotion to sneak around Darcy, but you just could not help yourself," Colonel Fitzwilliam said, leaning forward. "You saw his footing was precarious, and you took advantage."

Mr. Wickham sighed. "I may have accidentally brushed him as I passed. It is not my fault if he was unable to keep his feet."

Elizabeth's fury rose. Mr. Wickham might have killed Mr. Darcy that night. She might have lost the best chance she would ever have to love and be loved.

"Miss Elizabeth," said Mr. Picton appearing suddenly and lifting her hand to kiss it. "I have not seen you since that dreadful incident at the theatre. You saved Mr. Darcy's life that night, I am quite certain."

Colonel Fitzwilliam muttered something about having helped.

"Oh, do tell, Mr. Picton," Mrs. Farthington-Spit cooed. Elizabeth had forgotten for a moment that she was there. Mr. Picton walked the older woman away, already regaling her with the tale.

Elizabeth glanced back at her aunt and uncle. Aunt Gardiner smiled at Elizabeth, and Uncle Gardiner smiled at his wife.

Darcy was impressed with Elizabeth's family. When he turned back to speak with Elizabeth, his own aunt was staring at him.

She looked at Elizabeth, and then at him. Darcy knew exactly what she was telling him to do, and he shook his head at her.

Lady Matlock touched the earl's sleeve and whispered in his ear. He glanced up at Darcy, brows lifted. *Propose*, he mouthed.

No one had told Darcy this would be a part of the plan tonight, for if they had, he would never have agreed. His aunt wanted him to propose to Elizabeth? In public? It went against everything he held dear about keeping one's private life, well, private.

Lady Matlock tipped her head slightly to one side and glared at him. He glared back.

Then the Viscount saw that his parents were holding a silent conversation with his cousin. He met Darcy's gaze and shrugged.

Do what she asks, the shrug said. *There will be no getting around it anyway.*

Darcy closed his eyes for a moment. At least the music had been good.

"Are you well, sir?" Miss Elizabeth inquired.

"I ask for your pardon in advance."

"Why?"

"Cover your ears," he instructed her, and she did. He gave Milton a reluctant nod.

"*Attention!*" the viscount cried, immediately producing a stool, though from where, Darcy could not say.

Darcy reluctantly stepped up so that he towered over the entire room. "I cannot fathom why any of you might have an interest in this," he said with a scowl. "For it is certainly none of your business."

Several of the women gasped and some of the men laughed. They were ignored.

"However, as it appears that one night in my life last week appears to be more interesting to you than anything in your own, let me say for once and all—Miss Elizabeth Bennet is a woman of honour, of integrity, of bravery, and of virtue. Any man would have the greatest of fortune to have her agree to become his wife." He explained what had happened at the theatre for at least the hundredth time, and though there was some rumbling, no one contradicted him, not even Wickham, who was being held firmly in place by Fitzwilliam.

"I insisted Miss Elizabeth release her hold on my cravat because I feared she would be pulled down the stairs alongside me. But she refused." He laid out the events that had occurred on the road to Hunsford. "She did sprain her ankle—in a carriage accident. That was the truth, not a euphemism."

"A eupha what?" someone hissed.

Mr. Darcy grunted impatiently. "Finally, my aunt Lady Catherine is harbouring disappointments of a certain nature I am sure you can surmise," he said, directing his words most pointedly to a small gaggle of elderly ladies wearing wigs, "and wrote letters to her friends here in town that I suspect contained a great deal of vitriol and not much truth at all. There is no engagement, no marriage contract, no promise of any kind between her daughter and me, something I remind my aunt each year when I visit at Easter. My cousin does not want to marry me, and I would never force a woman to do so."

The viscount appeared with a second stool. "Mother has transformed me into her footman," he grumbled. "The story was not *that* bad." With a flourish, he set it down next to Darcy and handed Elizabeth up.

She was adorably flustered, so much so that she did not protest.

"I would never have married her, Elizabeth," Darcy said softly. "Even had she wanted me. For she is not you."

"I know," she said teasingly. "Agnes said as much."

Darcy grunted. Impertinent girl. He took her hands and raised his voice. "Miss Elizabeth Bennet."

Miss Elizabeth offered Darcy a barely perceptible nod, her eyes darting about the room.

Darcy's grasp on her hands tightened and her gaze returned to his. "This is not the proposal I planned, but I must tell you, here"—he lifted his eyes to the ceiling in such a sardonic manner that Elizabeth giggled lightly—"in front of our families, our friends, some slight acquaintances, and a number of complete strangers, that I *admire*, *respect*, and *love* you."

Her expression was all tenderness, and he was lost in her approbation for a moment before recalling himself to their audience. "Indeed," he continued, "I love you most ardently, and I beg you now to relieve my suffering and consent to be my wife."

Miss Elizabeth pressed her lips together before feigning innocence and asking, "You are suffering?"

"Elizabeth," he growled.

She smiled brightly. "I do consent to be your wife, Mr. Darcy," she said, speaking up so she was sure to be heard. "In fact, I am quite looking forward to it."

Chapter Eighteen

Mr. Darcy stepped down from the stool amid the crowd's chatter and laughter.

"Darcy is ever himself," the viscount said to a group of men Darcy recognised from his club. "Even when he is in a friendly crowd, he cannot help but insult."

The men all looked over at him with grins. Darcy grunted. He would never live this down. He helped Elizabeth to the floor.

"Cousin," Colonel Fitzwilliam said in wonder, still holding on to a smirking Wickham, "I would never have believed it of you. It is the very last way I would imagine you proposing. What happened to not forcing her to accept you?"

"Darcy always takes what he wants," Mr. Wickham said with a sneer. "He does not care that Miss Elizabeth despises him."

Colonel Fitzwilliam pretended to admire the knot in Mr. Wickham's cravat while giving the neckcloth a tight twist. Mr. Wickham coughed.

"Oh, you *are* behind the times, Mr. Wickham," Elizabeth said. "I was fooled at first, but a man's actions will always reveal his character more reliably than honeyed words."

"I suppose I have you to thank for my happiness, Wickham," Mr. Darcy said. "Had you been able to resist trying to harm me, Miss Elizabeth and I might not have resolved our misunderstandings so quickly and thoroughly."

Mr. Wickham's frown delighted Elizabeth. She turned to Colonel Fitzwilliam. "Have no fear for me or your cousin, sir. I did not feel in the least forced." Elizabeth glanced up at Mr. Darcy, and he lifted his shoulders slightly. "For he had already asked, you see. I accepted him before we entered the carriage tonight."

"Why did you offer a second time, then?" he asked Mr. Darcy, incredulous. "You might just have informed everyone that you were already engaged."

Mr. Darcy's answer was simple. "Because your mother insisted."

"When was this?" Elizabeth asked.

"It was in her eyes," he said. "She can speak quite emphatically with her eyes."

Colonel Fitzwilliam nodded in agreement. "There is no withstanding that look."

"It can be done," the viscount said. Then he winced. "But there are consequences." He picked up both stools and hurried away.

Mr. Darcy inclined his head towards Mrs. Farthington-Spit, where she was engrossed in whatever it was Mr. Picton was telling her. "Unless I miss my guess, your mother and Elizabeth's aunt intended that the papers would write about the fastidious Fitzwilliam Darcy making a public spectacle of himself because he is in love. Truly, it is better than anything Wickham might devise to sell them. She has put you out of business, Wickham."

"She will write that you are a secret romantic," Miss Elizabeth said cheerfully.

"Oh, that is not a secret in the family, not at all," Fitzwilliam said. "By the by, Darcy," he asked, shaking Mr. Wickham, "what would you like to do with this one?"

"I asked your mother to issue another invitation," Mr. Darcy said, raising his hand and beckoning a navy commander over from the other side of the room.

"Commander King?" he inquired.

The man nodded, and Elizabeth felt her lips turning up into a wide smile.

"I am pleased you could join us before collecting your niece in Meryton," Mr. Darcy said.

Mr. Wickham's complexion paled significantly.

"This the man who has been sniffing around Mary?" asked the commander, crossing two rather muscular arms across his chest.

"The very one, sir," Elizabeth confirmed. "He has, in fact, publicly announced their engagement."

"That is rather hasty, Mr. Wickham," Commander King snarled, "particularly as you arrived here with another woman entirely. Come," he said, taking a few steps forward, "I would like a few words."

Wickham jerked out of Fitzwilliam's grip and raced for the stairs.

"Thank you, Mr. Darcy," the commander said, and walked briskly after him.

Before the commander had even reached the railing, there was a scream and the sound of a falling body.

Everyone rushed the stairs, and Elizabeth, not being overly blessed with height, could not see what had happened.

"Mr. Darcy," she asked, "might you make use of your altitude on my behalf?"

Colonel Fitzwilliam reclined against the wall, tears trickling down his cheek as he laughed. "Never a man better served."

"Wickham has tripped over his own feet and fallen down the stairs in his rush to escape Commander King." Mr. Darcy leaned forward. "They are coming back up now."

The assembled patrons parted as the commander hauled Mr. Wickham back into the concert hall, two other naval officers now trailing behind them. Mr. Wickham was holding a handkerchief to his face. His nose was angled sharply to the right, and when he briefly lowered the white cloth, it was obvious he had lost at least one front tooth.

"Is he still the most beautiful man you have ever met?" Mr. Darcy asked.

She sighed and leaned into Mr. Darcy's side, relishing the feeling of his hand as it rested lightly on her lower back. "Alas, I believe that that title must now go to . . . the viscount."

"Elizabeth Bennet," Mr. Darcy said, half laughing and half exasperated, "when we marry, you will not be able to tease me with such impunity."

"Then I had better accomplish as much of it as possible before our vows are read," Elizabeth told him innocently.

"Another accomplishment you require, Mr. Darcy?" asked Lady Ellen, who had strolled over with Lady Ralston and Lady Slater. "My goodness. I am sure Miss Elizabeth is welcome to you!"

All three of them opened their fans with a unified flick of their wrists and laughed behind them as they strolled away.

"I do not know how they do that," Elizabeth said, shaking her head.

"What have you been saying?" Mr. Darcy growled.

Elizabeth smiled brightly. "Oh, the truth, Mr. Darcy. Only the truth."

Darcy slumped back against the squabs, exhausted.

"What an evening," Mrs. Gardiner said, and then added, "Lady Matlock is quite a wonder. Working with her has been great fun."

"She even managed to coax *two* proposals from Mr. Darcy here," Mr. Gardiner said glibly.

"Only the second, sir. The first was my own, and I am pleased, given how events this evening transpired, that I stole a moment to do it."

"So am I," Miss Elizabeth said quietly. "For some small part of me should always have wondered whether you had been forced to propose, and whether I, being in such a public place, had felt compelled to accept."

"Now there can be no regrets," Jane said cheerfully. "And despite the reason, Mr. Darcy, I did find your declarations to be quite romantic."

"Not you too, Miss Bennet," Darcy said with a groan.

"No, she is right, Darcy," Bingley said with a lilt in his voice that immediately put Darcy on his guard. "Quite dashing, really."

"Jane," Miss Elizabeth said slowly. She had noticed, too. "Do *you* have anything you would like to share with us?"

"Well," Miss Bennet began, then glanced at Bingley.

"While you were so busy drawing the attention of the entire room, Darcy, I offered Miss Bennet my hand, and she accepted me."

"The entire room was staring at you and Lizzy, so we had complete privacy," Miss Bennet said, staring happily at Bingley in the light of the lanterns hanging outside.

"It was perfect." Bingley smiled at Miss Bennet.

Darcy rubbed the back of his head. "You are welcome."

Congratulations and light laughter made their way around the coach's occupants.

"Thank goodness," Mr. Gardiner said when they were all done. "I shall finally be able to return to work! And next time you visit my offices, gentlemen," he added, "the earl has asked to accompany you. Wants to try to convince me to make him a silent partner."

They were quite a caravan when they arrived at Longbourn a week later, for despite having written to Mr. Bennet, neither Mr. Darcy nor Mr. Bingley had received replies, and they wished to speak with him as soon as might be arranged.

Mamma was speechless when their intendeds handed them down from Mr. Darcy's luxurious coach. "You are all welcome, of course," she said, wringing her hands, "but I do not understand why you are here."

"Lizzy, you will never guess," Lydia crowed. "Miss King has been taken away by her uncle to Liverpool, and Wickham is not to marry her after all!"

"Yes, Lydia," Jane said. "Lizzy and I are both aware."

"How could you possibly know?" Lydia asked, her bottom lip stuck out in a pout.

"Because we witnessed Commander King's confrontation with Mr. Wickham while we were in town," Elizabeth said. "Mary, Kitty," she said, kissing each sister on the cheek, "how have you been?"

"Well, thank you," Mary said. "It has been nice having the pianoforte to myself."

Elizabeth smiled. Mary would never change. "Well, soon enough you shall have it to yourself again, Mary."

"What does that mean, Lizzy?" Kitty asked. "Have you a beau?"

Mr. Darcy sighed, rather theatrically, she thought. "Am I so poor a suitor you cannot even recognize me as one?" he asked.

Elizabeth would forever recall the moment a single statement shocked all three of her younger sisters into silence at once.

After a few moments with Jane assuring Mamma that everything was as it should be, she waved them inside. "Come in, come in, you must refresh yourselves. You must stay for dinner, for Mr. Bingley is quite in my debt, you know. Mr. Darcy may stay too, if he will."

She had not heard a thing Mr. Darcy had said.

Elizabeth pressed Mr. Darcy's hand, but he shook his head at her. "Your mother is fine," he told her softly. "I cannot forget how Lady Catherine greeted *you*. This is nothing."

Her father was just now standing, laying a ribbon over the page of a book and turning the cover over, when she opened the door to his study a crack and peeked inside.

"Lizzy!" he said, thoroughly surprised. "Are you not meant to be in Kent for another month?"

"Papa," she said reprovingly. "Uncle Gardiner sent you at least three letters."

"And I am sure I would have read them eventually," Papa replied. "But as you are here, why do you not simply tell me?"

"No," she said, fond and irritated at once. "I have a guest, as does Jane. Perhaps you should find and read those letters before you join us. That way, you will not have missed anything important."

"Guests, eh? You have not brought back the Collinses, have you, my dear?"

"Read the letters, Papa. I will see you after."

Elizabeth closed the door behind her. She loved her father and always would. He had encouraged her walks, her childhood flights of fancy, her desire to learn everything that interested her. Well, within reason. But she had long known he was not a good husband and had never wished to marry a man like him.

Mr. Darcy, on the other hand, would make an excellent husband, a firm but loving father, and a passionate lover. Not that she really knew what all those heated looks meant, exactly, but Aunt Gardiner had made some humorous remarks about them. She also had some ideas of her own, and she was very, very anxious to learn.

After they were wed, of course.

The London papers—not only the *Examiner*—had been full of the news of Mr. Darcy's accidental scandal and romantic proposal, which made her betrothed only too pleased to remove from town.

And while there was no rush, not anymore, Elizabeth also did not wish for months to pass before they wed. Jane had waited long enough, and so had she.

A muted cry came from her father's book room, and Elizabeth smiled.

Epilogue

E lizabeth stood outside of Longbourn as Mr. Darcy's carriage came to a stop. A few moments later, he flashed a smile at her as he handed his sister down.

It had been a month since Mr. Darcy had proposed, and the final banns had now been called. They would be married in three days, and Elizabeth was all anticipation. Only one important introduction remained—the most important one, she believed.

Miss Darcy might have come to Hertfordshire earlier—she had certainly petitioned for it—but Mr. Darcy was adamant that his sister should remain at her lessons until he returned to London to collect the final marriage contract. Elizabeth had read it before it was sent off and had been struck anew by how truly generous a man her intended was.

When she had read the four sides of a closely crossed, enthusiastic letter of welcome from his younger sister, she could only surmise that generosity was a Darcy trait.

Miss Darcy was taller and larger than Elizabeth, her figure quite womanly despite her youth. Other than her light eyes, she was very much a feminine version of her brother.

"Miss Darcy," Elizabeth said cheerfully once the introductions were done, "I have been longing to meet you. I am so pleased you are here."

"Oh," the girl replied shyly, "I have been very much anticipating our meeting, Miss Elizabeth."

"None of that, now," Elizabeth teased. "We are to be sisters, so you must call me Elizabeth, or Lizzy, as my other sisters do."

Miss Darcy's expression was so full of longing that Elizabeth's heart went out to her at once. "Then you must call me Georgiana," the girl said.

"I shall," Elizabeth said, taking Georgiana's arm and leading her inside, "but you must be prepared for my sisters to convert you to George or Georgie almost immediately. No name of four syllables ever lasts long here."

Mr. Darcy's chuckle was soft and deep.

"Your brother laughs only because his Christian name is three syllables in length and is thus safe from truncation."

Georgiana giggled.

"I have missed you," Mr. Darcy whispered in Elizabeth's ear as Longbourn's butler took their coats.

"And I you," she replied quietly. "But you have returned with such a delightful sister for me that I shall not chastise you for being away a day longer than you promised."

"Georgiana," Mr. Darcy said, "would you like to refresh yourself before meeting your other sisters?"

His sister nodded and was shown to another room, leaving Elizabeth and Mr. Darcy alone in the hall.

"Forgive me for the delay," he said apologetically. "Wickham still believed he had the upper hand."

"What has been done with him, then?" she asked.

"Fitzwilliam has sent him to the regulars. He will serve under a commanding officer who is a close friend of my cousin's and has promised to send him quarterly reports. The regiment is posted as far north as one can go and still remain in England."

"You paid out a great deal of money for this, I suspect."

Mr. Darcy pulled a face. "I paid for his commission as an ensign and will pay for any promotions for which he is eligible, so long as he behaves. If he does not, I shall call in the debts of his which I hold—they are substantial—and he shall go to debtor's prison. Should he attempt to sell his commission before twenty years are up, the money will revert to me."

"I suppose that is the best way about it. Keep the carrot dangling before him like a donkey."

Mr. Darcy stepped back but took her hands in his own. "Wickham has ever been an opportunist. He had no plan that night at the theatre, he simply could not resist the chance to make me look foolish, even though it would have been better for his own interests to slip away into the crowd. Now that Wickham's looks are badly damaged, we were able to convince him that this arrangement is to his advantage. He wished for an allowance as well, but I disabused him of that notion."

Elizabeth huffed. "It galls me that you will pay anything at all. He has had more than his share from you."

Mr. Darcy nodded. "But the money will not be his for many years, and if he makes good and serves the country for that long, he is welcome to it. He will not be at liberty to bother us, which is all I want."

Georgiana reappeared, and Elizabeth smiled at her. Before she could speak with the girl, however, her youngest sister Lydia burst from the drawing room, dark curls bobbing wildly.

"Oh, there you are, Miss Darcy!" Lydia exclaimed. "We are in urgent need of your opinion, for Kitty says my new bonnet does my complexion no favours, but everyone knows her eye for such things is not half so good as mine."

"Lydia," Elizabeth said warningly.

"Oh," Lydia said, and bobbed a curtsy. "I beg your pardon. I am Miss Lydia Bennet, and we shall soon be sisters."

Georgiana had drawn her bottom lip in and was biting it. Not with shock or disdain, Elizabeth was relieved to note, but to prevent herself from laughing.

Lydia grabbed Miss Darcy's hand and tugged her into the drawing room. The door closed.

"I promise that although Lydia has no use for manners, your sister shall be quite safe," Elizabeth teased. "Jane and Mr. Bingley are inside." She took one of Mr. Darcy's hands in both of hers and lifted it to her lips.

Mr. Darcy glanced about and, finding them quite alone, stroked her cheek with his thumb and leaned down to place a kiss on her forehead. "Three days. Three days, and you shall be mine."

Elizabeth savoured the touch of her intended's lips on her skin before taking his arm and pointing them towards the closed door. "The papers may have called it an accidental scandal, Mr. Darcy," she said, and smiled at the sniff of contempt he could not prevent, "but I find that I shall always consider it a happy one instead."

The End

Want even more Darcy and Elizabeth? Click here for *An Accidental Scandal's* Bonus Epilogue!

(Or type this into your browser: https://BookHip.com/VWKMJXB)

Not interested in the Bonus Epilogue, but want to join Melanie's newsletter to vote on story elements, read excerpts of WIPs, or get news about upcoming publications? Scan or just go to her webpage for a sign-up link!

SCAN ME!

JOIN THE NEWSLETTER
WWW.MELANIERACHELAUTHOR.COM

About The Author

Melanie Rachel first read Jane Austen's novels as a girl at summer camp and will always associate them with starry skies and reading by flashlight. She was born and raised in Southern California but has also lived in Pennsylvania, New Jersey, and Washington. She currently makes her home in Arizona where she resides with her husband and their incredibly bossy Jack Russell Terrier.

Want updates on special giveaways and new books? Sign up for Melanie's newsletter at https://www.melanierachelauthor.com/newsletterand all her bonus content at https://www.melanierachelauthor.com/bonus-content. You can also find Melanie at www.melanierachelauthor.com or on Facebook and Instagram at *melanierachelbooks*.

Acknowledgments

As anyone who writes and publishes knows, authors don't get to the finish line on their own, and my mother always taught me to say thank you. So here we go . . .

Thank you to . . .

To my beta, cold, and ARC readers, those who pointed out errors or inconsistencies or just asked the right questions.

My critique partner extraodinaire, Sarah Courtney, who helps me write myself out of corners and makes me laugh.

Sarah Pesce of Lopt&Cropt editing, who always makes me consider things like structure, plot, and theme—even when I don't want to. Especially when I don't want to.

Author Elizabeth Adams, who laughed at *most* of the jokes.

Finally, thank you to all my readers. I'm so very grateful for you all.

Other Books by the Author

An Accidental Holiday

An Unexpected Inheritance

A Gentleman's Honor

Transforming Mr. Darcy

I Never Knew Myself

Drawing Mr. Darcy (duology)

Headstrong (trilogy)

Courage Requires

Courage Rises

Printed in Great Britain
by Amazon

40626680R00088